Aisles

Aisles

PAUL MAGRS

First published in Great Britain in 2003 by
Allison & Busby Limited
Bon Marche Centre
241-251 Ferndale Road
Brixton, London SW9 8BJ
http://www.allisonandbusby.com

A catalogue record for this book is available from the British Library

ISBN 0 7490 0656 0

Printed and bound in Wales by
Creative Print & Design

PAUL MAGRS is a lecturer in English Literature and Creative Writing at the Univerity of East Anglia. He is the author of five highly acclaimed previous novels, *Modern Love, Marked for Life, Does it Show?, Could it be Magic* and *All The Rage,* as well as a collection of short stories, *Playing Out.*

Funkymonkey and Iris

It was just as well Glenda didn't try to phone him that night. She was out later than she'd planned and he was waiting up. But he was distracted. Robin was otherwise engaged that night. He was upstairs in his study in their terraced house, plugging away at the computer. He was opening up little oblongs on the screen, neat windows into chatrooms. He had a number of them on the go at once.

Brazenhussy was oddly recalcitrant tonight and she was the one who usually held most interest for him. Neckrubslut was far too chatty as a rule, and he couldn't keep up with her. He was tempted to click her square off and send her that chilling message: 'Funkymonkey has left the room or is ignoring you.'

Funkymonkey was Robin's name. When he was Funkymonkey he came on like an animal: all teeth and hair and no holds barred. He claimed to be sitting shirtless or in his gymshorts, having just been working out in his private gym. That got them all worked up and clicking on his name in the East Anglian Chatroom. They'd be demanding private chats and asking for more specs.

PVT me, PVT me, they demanded.

Robin opened window after window to try out new voices, though he was loyal to Brazenhussy and Neckrubslut, of course. When he opened their boxes he thought it was just like having a doll's house. Peering in the windows to hear what they were saying. Under all the windows, layered, overlapping, he could still see the document he had been writing. In twenty-four point type – because his eyes were rubbed sore this late at night – were his notes for the thing he felt he ought to be writing. One click on any part of that fragmented text would shuffle it back up to the front. Instantly he'd be back to being who he should be. Funkymonkey no more.

His real self wasn't at all hairy and impetuous. His real self was concerned with magic and evil in the twentieth century novel. That's what Robin was thinking about, really, but only in patches, only in glimpses, all underlying the chats he was having with these women who were living – how close? Forty miles away? Twenty? Ten? Across town? The next street?

Neckrubslut was insisting: 'I don't know why we sit up all night like this. Why can't we do this in the daytime?'

It was coming on to four o'clock. Robin couldn't see himself sleeping at all tonight. He wanted to tell this woman just how absurd he'd feel writing messages to her in the daytime, with the two real, physical windows in his study open to the street, where real and ordinary things were going on. He wanted to say that he'd be ashamed, during those times, to have even heard of a person who called herself Neckrubslut. Even Brazenhussy wasn't so bad. She, he imagined, gave herself that name with a laugh, a wry chuckle. Her adopted persona would be one quite different to her waking self. Being Brazenhussy was escape for her. That was understandable, only natural.

Neckrubslut worried Robin somewhat, because the name spoke of someone being needy. Someone who was after – not illicit sex in person or sex on the phone or sex on-line … oh, heavens, not sex at all, even … But someone who was after just a rub. Just a rub on the neck. Just animal affection.

The more he thought of it, the more it gave him the horrors. This unseen woman out there, asking to be rubbed. And asking to meet up in the daytime some day. He knew she was working up to asking him again. She would go on about the excitement of meeting in the flesh and how different it would be, how human and odd.

When they asked this, Funkymonkey would always turn his ladies down.

They could be anyone. He had no wish to see them up close.

Tonight Brazenhussy was slow. Tonight she'd let the mask slip a little and she wasn't quite as brazen anymore. He typed in a line asking her why. This time she was quicker on the uptake. Her answer flashed back:

'Drunk. Typing slow. Very tired.'

But still here. Still doggedly logging on. Still seeing who else was in the room. Desperate not to be left out of it. To be one of the women around Funkymonkey through the night. Grooming his pelt, seeking his opinion. Flirting and trying to draw him out into the open, out of his cage. Indeed, Brazenhussy knew she was one of his favourites and so, drunk or not, she had to be there.

'Have you been out?' he asked.

'Oh yes,' she typed back. 'Out clubbing.'

Maybe she was younger than he'd thought. This surprised him. Disappointed him, too. He'd assumed these were all mature ladies. That thought had gratified him, obscurely.

11

That they could be mature and grownup and they could still force themselves awake through the wee small hours, just to chat with Funkymonkey. I'm the king of the swingers, he thought. And I'm running out of cigarettes.

He'd have to jog out down the road to the twenty-four-hour garage. He'd have to log off. Maybe he'd do it without warning and imagine all these women's sighs and groans as he abandoned them and the small window that represented him on their screens went dead and shut up shop.

Leave them wanting more.

He clicked off Neckrubslut and it gave him a twinge of satisfaction. Then he clicked off the newer ones, who were shy and hadn't lived up to the promise of their novelty. With more space clear he could see more of his notes on the document underneath.

It was a kind of 'What If?' thing. What if Virginia Woolf's Mrs Dalloway, while out on her run around the dark streets and squares of Bloomsbury during her mad night out ... what if she'd strayed too far? What if she'd shot right out of her orbit, propelled by her visions and neuroses, right across Charing Cross Road and into Soho? And what if, on that late Edwardian night, she'd been picked up by savage little chinamen armed with knives and nunchuckas and was carried off screaming into an underground den of vice? One that smelled rank and was steamy with opium fumes? What if they'd sold Mrs Dalloway down the sweating river to Limehouse and into the merciless talons of their master, Fu Manchu?

This was Robin's conceit that night. Virginia Woolf does slave trade slash fiction in a high-low modernist exploitation racket pastiche job. He'd had quite a laugh with it for a couple of hours (Mrs Dalloway dropping her flowers in the gutter as the wily chinamen picked her up and carried her, each holding a feebly struggling limb, high above their oily pigtailed heads). He had laughed and tapped away for quite a while till he hit a bad patch and cursed and wondered what the point of it was. And then he'd flung himself into the chatrooms and to the mercy of his faceless, friendly women.

Robin often found himself writing little fictions like this.

The revealed document made him feel depressed now. The flashing cursor at the end of the last word, mid-sentence, was like a mocking rebuke.

Only one window was still open: the tired and drunken Brazenhussy, who hadn't stirred her stumps to say anything more. Maybe she'd dropped asleep on her keyboard, face down on all the letters. He glanced at the dwindling list of names on the East Anglian Chatroom menu. They were popping off and crawling to their beds before dawn. And Mrs Dalloway was floating down the Thames to meet a wicked oriental genius. It's been a long night, Robin thought.

And no one new. No enticing new name was going to join the room now. He might as well stop and go out to get his fags and wait for Glenda to show up at last.

At that very moment a new member's name appeared.

Iris Murdoch had joined the room.

Very neat and plain, her name added itself to the bottom of the list.

13

Robin blinked and rubbed at his short, dark beard.

In the main, shared chatroom the newcomer was typing her first message.

'Hullo room. Say hullo to Iris Murdoch.'

Robin swallowed.

He sat back on his computer chair (a present from Glenda. A specially-designed one, for his back.) He took his hands off the keys. He let Brazenhussy push forward and answer first.

'Hi, Iris Murdoch. You know, really, you oughtn't to use your real, whole name. You should choose a made-up name, like mine. You don't think Brazenhussy is really my name, do you?'

Robin found himself laughing. Brazenhussy – drunk as she was tonight – had given herself away as young and silly. He hoped she wasn't one of his own students. Quickly, he typed: 'I think "Iris Murdoch" is actually a made-up name, Brazen. "Iris Murdoch" is a deceased novelist. She wrote lots of novels and died of Alzheimers in 1999.'

He clicked 'send' with a peculiar satisfaction. Fuck it, if it didn't sound much like Funkymonkey. If it sounded more like Robin's dry, habitual, lecturing tone.

'Oh,' wrote Brazen. 'Right. Sorry, Iris Murdoch.'

Almost immediately, Iris Murdoch replied. 'Don't apologise. You meant well, Brazenhussy. And you are quite right. I should have used a pseudonym. I'm new to all of this, as you might have guessed.'

14

Robin wondered about pulling his usual Funkymonkey stunt, as he would with any unwitting newcomer. Usually he would click on them for a private chat; abrupt, assertive, making sure they knew who was in charge around here. But Brazenhussy was asking: 'Are you really a novelist then?'

He sighed. The girl was a cretin.

Iris Murdoch shot back: 'I was. For a very long time I used to make up all sorts of things and write them down in exercise books, copying them out again and again. Someone else would do the typing. I was never very good at that. I'm having some trouble using this keyboard here tonight.'

Brazenhussy said: 'I think you're doing very well. Are you here to get ideas for a new novel? I bet you'd get some good ideas here.'

'For god's sake...' Robin moaned. Quickly, in his private window for Brazen, he typed: 'She's having you on, you silly mare.' Then he clicked Iris Murdoch's name roughly, twice, for a private consultation.

'Hullo,' she typed, in the top left hand corner of the blank box. Then she added, 'Hullo, Funkymonkey.'

'Why are you calling yourself Iris Murdoch?' he wrote.

Her reply came very swiftly. It was a simple question mark.

'No one here will get the joke,' he replied.

'You did, Mr Monkey,' she said.

'Are you a big Iris Murdoch fan?' he asked. 'Is that it?'

'I never really liked to read my own work,' she said. 'It was never quite what I expected it to be. What I had meant it to be. But you would understand about that, wouldn't you?'

Robin stared and his fingers hovered uncertainly over the keys. He wasn't sure where to go next with this. He couldn't very well ask her the usual stuff, like what she was wearing, and so on. What would she say?

He wondered if, at last, he'd found someone genuinely mad.

'Come off it,' he typed brusquely. 'It's not even funny. Iris Murdoch is dead.'

He waited with his mouth open, to see how she would react to this flash of stark realism.

'Iris Murdoch has left the room or is ignoring you.'

'Fuck!'

He stood up.

'Bollocks.'

He disconnected the whole thing in a fit of pique. The bitch had blanked him, whoever she was. He pulled on his shoes crossly and thundered down the stairs and out of the house to the garage.

* * *

That's when he was buying his cigarettes, and meeting Darren from work in the middle of the night and then Darren was telling him about a car accident he'd seen. And, later still, when she eventually came home from her night on the town, it turned out Glenda had seen the same wreck. It was all too late and too confusing. They'd gone to bed. Glenda had been looking after the fella whose wife had died. She was assuming responsibility, taking him under her wing. Robin didn't ask too many questions. He was just glad she was back. But the next day she was gone again, still helping out. Helping and shoe-horning the poor bereaved bloke back into his own life. Taking him home. Staying with him. And Robin was left alone. Left alone all Saturday to fend for himself.

He didn't think much about the death stuff. He didn't try to see what Glenda had seen, or try to imagine it all through her eyes. Friday night, the two of them had looked pretty shaken up. Robin had kept a respectful distance. Even imaginatively. He'd held onto Glenda in bed this morning and there were all these new sights and sounds and smells inside her, that she'd stored up through a whole, long, nightmarish time. They were things Robin would never really know about. She'd been some place without him and he was glad.

Realism.

Left alone, Robin dozed for much of Saturday night, catching up with himself. Glenda had gone out with Tony to help him sort things out. Robin woke up headachey, finding all the lamps left on and the daylight starting to drain out of the sky. He made strong, gritty coffee and wandered about the house in his boxer shorts and t-shirt. He felt as if he was looking for something and couldn't quite decide what it was. Then he realised it was Glenda he was looking for. He needed to talk to her. Not about anything special or in particular. He just needed everyday, time-filling chit-chat, to reassure him that he was in the right time and place and that real life was still going on.

That was a selfish thought, mind. When you bore in mind what was happening to Tony. Nothing would ever be the same for him. Hey, I should count my blessings, Robin thought. That's what I should do. I should just sit on that settee and fill up time counting all my blessings. But he racketed around the hollow house for a while, defiantly not getting dressed. He put on Dylan's *Bringing it All Back Home*, loud enough so he could hear it in every room of the house, then he trotted up to the study and downloaded his email. Might as well, he thought easily, though it was guaranteed to piss him off and it would make him, he knew, check out the little windows and the women again. Seeing as he was connected he may as well. It wouldn't cost much more, just to have a little swoop down, a little look into their rooms.

He sat resting his heavy head on his hands as the subject headings flashed up. A few routine circulars from departmental secretaries (the search for missing coursework, external examiners, plagiarists). A couple of demands for references from postgrads (relevant forms happily available as untranslatable attachments) and a couple of postgrads themselves, worrying over their research (its validity, its progress, its lateness). Some of his PhD students could be rather pushy and demanding. Then he blinked and saw that there was one email from an address he didn't recognise. Robin had a great, almost autistic memory for email addresses.

ThegreatI.M@underthenet.co.uk

Heedlessly, and knowing full well he shouldn't open mysterious parcels in case they contained viruses (Glenda had explained this to him patiently. Her explanation had made him think of Quatermass: unwrapping the mysterious package, unleashing unnameable horror on a very 1950s England ...) He opened the email anyway. Just four lines.

'Are all the books in the world made up at the same time?

In a place that is not here?

What were they up to when they wrote those books?

Were they up to bad things?'

Before Robin knew it, he had asked the machine to print it.

While the paper clunked and whirred, he was trying to convince himself that some student must have sent it. It was some daft theoretical thing translated from the French. Or maybe something out of a South American short story. Or from a novel by a British woman writer, one with a taste for aphorism and surrealism, and who, in her spare time, read South American short stories and French theorists in ropey translation. Probably one of his keener students had found it and thought he'd like it. But, if it was a quotation, there was no attribution. And the student didn't identify themselves.

It wasn't from a student.

He read the four lines again.

They made of him think of that thing EM Forster had written in *Aspects of the Novel*. About the big room somewhere outside of time, where all the writers of time past, present and future were writing all the books in the world and all at the same time. He'd imagined this as a white, circular, marble room, and everyone sitting very quietly, working very seriously, on hard stools. Cats and dogs made out of paper went padding back and forth, whispering and eager for attention. That was just how he'd imagined it. A very dry kind of place. It was an absurd image, Robin had always thought. It didn't allow for influence; for the natural, ongoing way that people read each other down through the generations; hijacking, smuggling, rewriting each others' forms and ideas.

And what did 'bad things' mean anyway? What bad things could the writers have been up to? He shivered involuntarily.

And looked back at the unfamiliar email address.

ThegreatI.M@underthenet.co.uk

He laughed aloud suddenly.

Then he was opening up the Internet and his usual chatrooms, drumming his fingers impatiently on the desktop as he waited to whizz through all the welcoming paraphenalia.

It was very slow this tea-time. He was used to it being very much quicker. He was used to logging on to this in the wee small hours. That was when he talked to his faceless ladies.

It was her.

It had to be her.

She was sending him silly gnomic messages to his everyday email address. Somehow she had got hold of his work email and now she was stalking him. Robin found himself vaguely stirred and thrilled by the idea. He was at a loss to know why. Tapping in his ID, his password, scrolling down the dizzying list of chatroom options ...

He crashed into his usual room and felt just as if he was dashing into a real, physical room, with coat-tails flying, hair awry, breathing heavily, eyes darting about the place.

It was almost empty. Much more sedate than he was used to. Someone called Bizzylizzy and another called Franky.

'Hi Funkymonkey!' typed Bizzylizzy, before he'd had a chance to do anything. He sat back in his orthopaedic chair and reflected briefly on how strange a place the East Anglian room was, without the likes of Brazenhussy and Neckrubslut. Bizzylizzy had clicked on for a private chat in the same abrupt, demanding way that Funkymonkey always did. The woman had barely said hello to him and now she was telling him the size of her bazooms and the colour of her nipples and hair, how she liked it rough and was looking for a meet with a view to a good hard shag in the early evening.

Robin was scandalized.

He typed to the depleted room at large: 'Has Iris Murdoch been in?'

And they didn't have an answer for that.

He said 'Shit' under his breath. He was making Funkymonkey look distinctly uncool. Iris was managing to spoil the poise his netpresence had so carefully built up. Funkymonkey was becoming as flustered and feckless as Robin himself often was.

He withdrew quickly from East Anglia One and went to look at the profiles of the members who regularly went there. This was something he never usually consulted. For some reason he had no interest in seeing the photos of themselves that Brazenhussy and Neckrubslut might have posted. Of course, he thought, that would spoil the fantasy and that's why I don't look. Of course, of course, the fantasy is the main thing. It's paramount. That's why I do it. I have such a rich, rewarding fantasy life. Such a vivid inner life. And it would puncture it quite badly, to see from their photos (they would bound to be terrible amateurish snaps) that the women of my dreams are clapped-out, ordinary tarts.

Sometimes Robin's thoughts surprised even him. Women of my dreams? Is that what they are to me? Is that what I want them to be?

Those were Funkymonkey's dreams, surely.

And Funkymonkey was a law unto himself, that was true enough. Where Funkymonkey's chatty libido led him was Funkymonkey's business and privilege and all Robin could do was follow on, flabbergasted and fascinated.

His heart jumped then because he had found Iris Murdoch's profile page. She actually had one! Last night's little visit hadn't been a one-off. And neither had it been some three-in-the-morning lowest-ebb hallucination on Robin's part. Here was her page in all its tidy glory, giving away just a little information. Just enough to get the basics across and give its owner a small stake in the elaborate East Anglian dating game.

There wasn't a photo at the top. It was a cropped version of the National Portrait Gallery postcard of Iris Murdoch. The painting from the back of the old Penguin paperbacks, Robin noted: the one in which Dame Iris looks every inch the Dame. With a severe but clear-eyed gaze and the springy leaves of some hothouse plant almost brushing up against her face, the rounded collars of her blue blouse echoing the shape of the leaves. And her hair looked like she'd cut it herself with the kitchen scissors.

It was Iris all right.

Underneath, in ten point script and terse, notational prose, she asked for 'no time-wasters, please' and claimed that she was a 'voluptuous, non-smoking, grey-haired writer and philosopher, rumoured to have died of Alzheimers some years previously.'

But she was still up for chat and a few laughs, regardless.

Almost as an afterthought a line had been tagged on the end:

'Saucy chat or Platonic dialogue – the choice is ours.'

Robin laughed and printed that page as well.

I'm losing my tiny fucking mind, he thought.

*****

'Hey, room. Say hi to Funkymonkey. The monkey's back in the room.'

'Hi, Funkymonkey.' Neckrubslut was the first one on his case.

He scrolled down the menu and saw that there were sixteen persons here, some he didn't recognise. He watched his own alias appear as the most recent incumbent.

'Everyone happy and ready for fun?' he typed.

'As ever!' said Neckrubslut.

'Hiya, Funkymonkey.' This was Brazenhussy. Reliable as ever. 'You clicked off last night without saying goodbye. What was wrong with you?'

'A monkey's got to do what a monkey's got to do. I can't pander to you ladies all night.'

'Isn't it spelled 'panda'?' asked Neckrubslut.

'I have to spread myself around,' typed the monkey.

'I wouldn't mind seeing you spread yourself round here,' said Brazenhussy. 'When's it going to happen, Funky?'

He started to reply, but was interrupted by them.

'He's all talk,' Neckrubslut put in.

'No trousers,' said Brazen.

'Stringing us along,' said someone else he'd never heard of in his life.

'One days, ladies,' he typed quickly, trying to reassert control, 'I'll come among you all.' He sent it. He followed it up with, 'Is that what you want, anyway? Do you want to spoil all our virtual fun? Do you really want actual fun? I didn't think you did.'

Brazenhussy replied in capitals. 'JUST GIVE ME SOME REAL ACTUAL FUN, YOU HAIRY QUIM-TEASING TOSSER.'

Robin laughed aloud. Then his heart skipped when he saw that Iris Murdoch had joined the room.

'Hullo room, say hullo to Iris.'

'Hiya, Iris.'

'Evening, Iris.'

Funkymonkey went straight to work. 'Excuse us, room. I'm asking Iris for a PVT. I may be gone for some time.'

There was a scandalized hush from his faceless ladies. You could measure it in the blinking of the cursor. No one was coming back at him. 'Ms Murdoch? Is that okay?' he asked, much more tentatively than the monkey ordinarily would.

Almost immediately a fresh box sprang up, superceding everything else on the screen.

'Hello,' appeared at the top.

'Hello, Iris. I got your email.'

'Good.'

'And I looked up your profile page. Very nice. Didn't you have a more recent picture?'

'Not really.'

'So ...' For a second Robin was stuck. He found himself writing, 'What are you wearing?'

'An old cardy. Tweed skirt. You?'

'I'm in my pyjamas. Marks and Sparks.'

'Very nice. I like men in proper pyjamas.'

'I didn't really understand your email. It was a little obscure.'

'Oh dear. I didn't mean it to be. I thought you'd be interested.'

'I am! I'm very interested.'

'Well, good.'

'You were talking about all the books in the world and their ... interconnectedness ...'

'Just something I've been thinking about. How you can wander off one page, straight into another ...'

'But what did you mean about 'bad things', Iris? You asked if all those writers, writing at the same time, are up to bad things?'

'Black magic. The Occult. Sorcery. I think they are. I think they're doing all sorts like that. Probably tapping into something. When you set the imagination going, you don't know what you're going to get back.'

'That doesn't necessarily mean bad.'

'It means it could be. It could also be good.'

'You need to explain more, Iris.'

'I know. But we're filling up our little box, and the other ladies are clamouring for you, Mr Monkey.'

'I need to know more.'

'I know.'

'Tell me more.'

'If you think of novels, those characters and situations exist without you reading them, don't they? They're just waiting for you to read them. They're waiting to get into your mind and be reformed inside there, forming a skin amongst your other cells. Another layer.'

'And they're there for all time?'

'Unless the cells die. Unless you have black spaces opening up in your mind.'

He paused then. 'That happened to you, didn't it?'

'They X-rayed me. I've read about it since. There were holes in my brain. Like cheese, Mr Monkey. Like old net curtains.

That was the space I had that was filled by my most private thoughts and inventions and all my adventures.'

'At least they're in your books.'

'Now they can form skins inside other people's minds. Yes, I know. It was ... believe me ... a very palpable transfusion.'

'You remember everything now?'

'I think so.'

'You do?'

'I believe so. When I try. It takes as much effort as thinking – any real, serious thinking ever did. But I do think now that some restoration goes on, somehow.'

'Where are you, Iris?'

'It feels very much like the Irish sea. Honestly, it does. A stormy night forever. I'm on a small ferry, its deck all greasy with rain. There is thunder and lightning going on all night and it never stops. It's chilly and damp, but I sit in the lounge – which is rather pleasant – and I have this laptop, which took a while to master. We're being tossed to and fro on the high seas. When the lightning flashes ... well, that's when I remember the most.'

'There are others there with you? You've got company?'

'Indeed I have. I think maybe that's what I meant when I said all the novelists of the world occupy one small space. Here it's mostly those who were busy scribbling in the nineteen-thirties, -forties, -fifties, -sixties. That terrible

28

breed. All of us chatting together and exerting our feeble wills.'

'On a ferry in a storm on the Irish sea?'

'Why not? It's as good a place as any to be. Just the other night Angus Wilson was disputing the location with me. (The same night. I think it's all the same night, really.) He was attempting to navigate by the stars. He was out on the deck with his white hair streaming out in the wind. His face - pink as tinned meat - gazing up. But the constellations here are fanciful. I think they dance around to confuse us. There's no captain, no crew to tell us where we are. We just muddle along. Squabbling and chatting and making further things up.'

'That's amazing,' said Robin. Lamely, he realised.

'Why do you need to know where I am?' she asked brusquely.

'I need to know where the words are coming from. I need a place for you to be in my head.'

'The words are not enough?'

'No.'

'You have to imagine me?'

'I think so. I can see you on that ship now. I want to know more.'

'You are greedy, I think, Mr Monkey.'

'I know.'

'But you don't need to know where your other, faceless ladies are, do you? You'd rather not know at all. You don't want or need them to be palpable and real.'

'No.'

'I wonder why not. I wonder what the difference is.'

'Because ...'

'Iris Murdoch has left the chat room or is ignoring you.'

The small oblong of their talk froze at that point.

Because ... he had wanted to say ... because I don't think I believe in you.

You have got to be fake.

But I don't want that. I want you to be real.

*****

Maybe I'm being stalked, Robin was thinking.

He was on the comfy chair he'd installed in his office. There was no one knocking at his door just now and he was free to close his eyes for a bit, even thought there was loads he had to do. Then the thought came to him, that the whole thing was a massive, miserable hoax. Someone, some evil soul was pretending to be Iris for him. They were luring him into some mad world where he lost all sense of proportion and they could laugh at him. Just laugh in his face, being a gullible old fool. It wouldn't be that hard. He'd already talked to her as if she was real.

This was the time of day on a Monday that he set aside for reading. Just reading and nothing else. There was a heap of drafts of essays to look at and a sector meeting coming up at lunchtime. He should really read the documentation for that. Being unprepared was how the other bastards got things past you. But, bugger it: reading was part of what he did, and what he was here to do. He needed to oil the old cogs somehow and it might as well be new oil. He had a black bag from Waterstone's on his desk, with a couple of new novels inside, both published by graduates of the writing program here. Robin prided himself on keeping up with what was going on. The two of them had been well-received in the papers' books pages yesterday: two more successful alumni to add to three decades' worth. One of the books belonged to a genre apparently known as Chicklit. It was a rewrite of *Portrait of a Lady*, with a contemporary swing: settings transposed from America, London, Venice, to Blackpool, Edinburgh, Kilburn. It was supposed to be filthy. The other book was a history of twentieth-century aesthetics as narrated by a parking meter.

Our alumni are smart cookies, Robin thought. They're really pushing the envelope. He only taught the writing program people when they joined in his Post-War Fiction course and there they proved they were brimming with things to say. He remembered these two writers from his seminars; how he'd thought of them as budding, back then. They had worn black outfits and said pertinent things thoughout, from the Writer's point of view.

Smart, smart cookies, he thought and left the books in their fresh bag. If he kept the receipt he could claim it back on research expenses. He had his copy of Iris's *The Sea, The Sea* resting on the bobbly arm of his chair. But that remained closed as he went on thinking about the possibility of a stalker on campus. We're very vulnerable here, he thought. Anyone could come knocking at that door, expecting to ask me absolutely anything, demand any kind of mentoring. Only this morning, at five-to-nine precisely, he'd had a visit from a very alarming-looking boy with multiple piercings and a winsome manner. He'd been going on about his dissertation on Katherine Mansfield. He was going to unearth the lesbian subtext in *Bliss*.

'But there isn't one!' Robin had said.

And the boy had looking pityingly at him.

'It's the inverse of Forster,' Robin was told. 'Just as all the women in Forster are men in drag, all the men in Mansfield are … um, women in drag.'

'Are you sure about this?'

'Quite sure,' said the boy. 'It's a Queer reading.'

Which meant – What I say, goes. Robin knew better than to quibble with that. They were all of them looking to unearth something, he thought. All of them were shuffling the old pages, wanting to boil things down and reveal the untold story. That's what we've taught them, he supposed. All these children take that kind of suspicion in their stride. They've got a nose for it. They're all ferretting out bad faith, if not cant.

It was terrifying to him, when he thought about it. For years he had encouraged students to look for the shadow story underneath the work, and now he found himself wanting to tell them to enjoy the writing for what it was. To revel in the fact of its simply being there, existing to be read.

His students looked at books (texts, they were texts) warily and expertly, like members of a bomb disposal squad. They roped off the area, got the feeble-minded and middle-browed to stand clear of the spot and then, in a controlled space, detonated the text. And bang: there goes Katherine Mansfield's lesbian subtext in all its glory, flung like a garter belt. Here's Kafka's morbid fear of his father. There's Byron's secretly-harboured career as a disco diva.

They were so professional, these youngsters.

Then he thought: the General Secretary sticks up all our home addresses and phone numbers and email addresses on the general office notice board. Should they fancy it, anyone could contact us at any time of day or night. They could bring that frighteningly blithe aptitude for deconstruction round to our front doorsteps whenever they fancied it.

No wonder he was getting maddening, obscure emails from someone claiming to be Iris Murdoch.

This, of course, was spoiling the whole of his fantasy dialogue with her. How had they known, anyway, that he had a secret life as Funkymonkey in the chatrooms of East Anglia? No one knew that. No one guessed the link between the monkey and his secret identity.

No, it surely couldn't be anyone here. He had printed out the text of all his conversations with the faceless dame already. Just in case.

There was a postcard of her, on the wall opposite his chair. It was tucked away in a corner of his collage of postcards of writers through the ages. His eye flicked to it now, unconsciously. She was right between TS Eliot and DH Lawrence. She was young in the photograph, crouched on the floor in a rumpled skirt and white blouse, her hair tangled up and her eyes striking. She looked boyish, truculent, determined, and as if she had lost something under the bed. She was a feisty androgyne, staring at him through the years and across the narrow space of his office, defying him not to believe in her.

He went out then. He went to stomp along the corridor to fetch some coffee, to see signs of life and to stop thinking about dead writers. He bumped straight into Darren, coming back from the general office, red in the face and holding his post as if he wanted to chuck it out as soon as possible.

'Funny thing,' Robin said, as first years swam by. 'When I saw you on Friday night in the twenty-four-hour garage ...'

'Oh yes?' asked Darren, not greatly interested.

'You were telling me about the car you and your friend had discovered. And about the dead woman you found at the wheel.'

Darren glanced left and right, as if it were a shameful secret. Really, he was being absurd. 'Yes?'

'Well, she was a colleague of my wife, Glenda. Glenda went out to identify the body, that very night.'

'Really?'

'Isn't it strange? The way it overlaps?'

Darren didn't really have his mind on the conversation, Robin could see.

'But isn't it a funny coincidence?'

Darren looked at him. 'Your Glenda had to identify her?'

'She went with the husband. She was quite shaken by it all.'

'I'm not surprised.'

'So we all link up,' said Robin. 'Somehow. We're all drawn together along lines of ... lines of something or other ...'

'Was she a friend of your wife's?'

'Not really,' said Robin. 'As far as I could make out. But she knew her, anyway. Said the woman worked on the delicatessen counter.'

Darren had queued for things, had asked for things and had bought them at that counter. He might have been served by the dead woman. He said so.

Robin shuddered and grinned suddenly, to lighten the atmosphere. 'Well, this is all a bit too Low Mimetic for me,' he chuckled. 'We're getting sentimental about a car crash victim off the deli counter. That's far too much Realism for this time of day.'

'Some of us quite like Realism,' said Darren.

'I forgot it was your chosen mode.'

'Middle-brow as it might be.'

'I never said that,' said Robin, in mock protest.

'But you make it sound like a default position. Like vanilla is to ice cream or to sex. Something you can always fall back on, if you lack imagination ...'

Robin's eyes widened. It wasn't like Darren to have an outburst in the corridor.

'It was your generation,' Darren was saying, 'who made Realism a dirty word. It was you lot who wanted everything to be zippy and all post-structuralist. A world where it didn't matter if the woman off the deli counter had died horribly. Because – look! She can come back to life! She can turn into a fish! It didn't matter because it wasn't real. She was just a heap of dead, hackneyed discourses and cooked meats and imported cheeses ...'

'Steady,' said Robin.

'But she was real, Robin. She was a real woman. She wasn't in a book and she hadn't written one, but she still mattered.'

'Hang on,' said Robin. 'I never meant ...'

But Darren had stepped back into his own office and closed the door on him. Robin stared at the mass of papers pinned to the door, looking for something that would signal to his embarrassed, jaundiced eye that lovely phrase, 'a mocking rebuke.'

But there was nothing.

He left Darren to his sulk and went to wrestle with the new and very complicated coffee machine, reflecting that, once someone had decided to valorize middle-brow sentimentality, there was no arguing with them. The high ground would always be theirs.

Darren was queer and from a working class background, to boot. Really, in the climate, he couldn't lose. Everything must be so clear-cut for him. He had everything on his side.

He should try being Robin for a change! Old, straight, married, dried-up, stalked, angry, defeated and deluded. How about that for a combo?

Robin took his espresso black and thickly sugared and contented himself that it was a nightmare being him.

Email when he got back. Little pinging noise from the machine. He clicked it up immediately.

'It's not a nightmare. It's not a dream, either. Calm down, Robin. You'll give yourself a fucking heart attack. Love, Iris. XXX'

*****

'We do bad things,' Iris was typing. 'That's what I was telling you, just the other night, Mr Monkey. That's our stock-in-trade. 'We do bad things, inflicting them on good, bad, indifferent people. We put them under pressure and we see how they react.

'They're a puzzle to us. We want to understand why they carry on like they do. We have no kind of expertise, other than in the ways that people carry on.

37

'We want to show them at their best and at their worst and we want to understand everything in between.'

'Yes,' Robin told her. 'I think I get that. I understand that.'

'Of course,' she said. 'You have read a lot of novels. That's no guarantee of understanding them, of course. You read them professionally and systematically, and that's how you analyse them. I'm coming at this from quite a different point of view.'

Now this irked him. 'You're coming broadcast live from a ferry stranded on the Irish Sea. You're like Radio Caroline in the Sixties. You're a pirate novelist. Or have you moved on now?'

'No, indeed,' she wrote. 'We're still here.

'I'm still tapping away on this silly, tiny, toylike keyboard, reliant on something called a modem to maintain my link with you. My only link with the physical world.

'(Don't you think a laptop is like a toy piano? Its notes tinny and callow-sounding?)
'Outside the storm is worsening, I think. That's the only index of time, of things progressing.

'The sea is wild, wild, wild tonight.'

Describe it, he wanted to tell her.

Describe that sea to me now, as you do in your novels. Make it real. Make it new.

As it was, Iris wasn't doing much descriptive work at all.

It was other business she had with him tonight.

'"Professional novelist" always seemed oxymoronic, as a term, to me at least,' she typed. 'We're all amateurs here, aboard this ship.The few of us still talking to each other, are agreed on this.

'Those of us who haven't squabbled and are now studiously ignoring one another have talked about this and are agreed that, writing as we do is a symptom of our inability to engage with the world of professions.

'With the world itself, perhaps.

'In your world people are very keen on everything being professional these days, aren't they? Codes of practise, transparency, accountability, being subject to review.What wonderful phrases! Everyone, everything, subject to review!

'All of you in glass houses. Nothing difficult or opaque.

'To me, a review is a smudgey couple of stunted columns – rancorous, fond, quibbling, admiring perhaps. But the sort of thing that I never read much of anyway.

'Tell me something, Mr Monkey. When did everything become so organised and grim?'

It was rhetorical, he knew.

She went on. 'None of us aboard this vessel would qualify for that world, I think. We'd fall at every hurdle. But we're all very old-fashioned. We oughtn't fit in. We ought to date.

'The world has moved on. Do you know, Virginia is so depressed with your world, that each night she flings herself into the foaming sea, just before dinner? It's a kind of mania with her. Or a hobby.

'She does it while we're having drinks each evening, regular as clockwork, and we take turns to fish her out again.

'As you may know, I'm a very strong swimmer. I'm a robust woman of a certain age with powerful arms and lungs. I was very given to braving the rivers, streams and seas when alive in your natural world.

'Starkers and undaunted, I could pull a few strokes.

'So, often it's me who gets roped in to fling off my cardigan and jump in the sea after poor, skinny Virginia. She weighs hardly anything, but some evenings she puts up quite a fight. I believe she weighs down her pockets with volumes of her journal.'

Robin was trying to picture it.

'The others are all either lazy or timid. Morgan Forster, Angus and Christopher, all standing there, wringing their hands: "We're not jumping in after her!" I tell them, "She's your friend! Not mine!"

'But they won't jump. That's what you get for hanging about with shipload of nancies, Mr Monkey. That's what they are. Finks and nancies.

'Noel won't even come out to watch, when Virginia pulls one of her stunts. He's still tinkling away on the Baby Grand

40

in the cocktail lounge. Still crafting those oh-so-sharp ditties of his. He won't write fiction any more. He claims to be put off by the presence of so many luminaries. The bristling of our collective unconscious, he says, gives him the right royal pip.'

'This is just gossip,' Robin sent back tersely. 'I'm not very interested in what Noel thinks. It's you I'm interested in, Iris.'

'Well, that's very flattering, Mr Monkey. I'm a fool for that these days.'

'Tell me again about the bad things, Iris. What is it you do that is so bad? You write, or wrote, fiction. These aren't real people you inflict your ideas and fantasies upon.'

'No?'

'You made them all up.'

'And so I have the right to do with them as I will?'

'I mean, they aren't real. It doesn't matter what you do. All your tortured intellectuals running around after unsuitable women and never getting to the end of their work, your doughty ladies of uncertain means, your wraithlike girls coming in to speak the truth ... They aren't real people!'

'Oh no?'

'No.'

'I see.'

Was she in a huff with him? Would she ignore him and leave the chatroom? He was determined to get in there first and to make her stay.

'Surely you never thought your characters were like real people? That was never the point, was it? Lifelikeness? They were in your own pocket universe, just as the characters invented by your shipboard companions occupied their own, respective pocket universes. And there they were subject to their own peculiar conditions... I mean, if one met any of your characters in real life, they'd make your hair stand on end.'

'Mr Monkey, the people I met in what you fondly call real life made my hair stand on end anyway.'

'Fair point.'

'We are still doing bad things. Even here in our reduced circumstances, even while on this tumultuous cruise...'

'You're still writing books?'

'Oh, of course. We write and rewrite the same ones forever. I've already told you that. But the real work goes on. The work that involves putting pressure on the character, on the real life subject ...

'We've broken out, Mr Monkey. Like the influence of a black magic cult. We dream up things to happen and we sit back to watch the results ...'

'On who?' he asked. 'Who do you watch?'

'Iris Murdoch has left the room, or is ignoring you.'

Robin was used to this now, her abrupt entrances and exits, and he didn't take them to heart any more. Probably something else had snagged her attention. He couldn't expect to have her all to himself.

When he went through to the bedroom, Glenda was still awake and he was surprised by this.

'I know you weren't working,' she said.

He was in the patch of light from the open door.

'We have to talk about this,' she said.

'About what?' He knew how defensive he sounded.

'Why you're staying up through the night, every night. Why you disturb my sleep like this. Who you're talking to through there. Who it is that takes up all this time.'

'Oh.' He started to undress.

'I'm sick of it, Robin. I can't sleep. I need to sleep.'

'I'm sorry if I'm keeping you awake. I didn't know. I'm...'

'I should have said something to you before. But it's driving me crazy, you staying up all night. Why don't you, why can't you come to bed with me? I'm your wife.'

He laid down his warm shirt on the chair and sat to unlace his shoes. 'I'm onto something. And it is to do with work. Really, it is.'

She couldn't see his face properly now. He undid his

trousers and let them drop. He stood there still, unwilling to move.

'We have to talk about this, Robin.'

'All right.'

'I'm putting pressure on you, I know.'

'Pressure,' he said dully.

'But you don't tell me anything. You're like a closed book. But I'm only putting pressure on you because I love you. Because I feel the pressure too.'

He paused and she heard and felt, rather than saw, his creeping closer to the bed.

'Budge up,' he told her. 'We will talk, I promise. But not tonight. Too tired tonight. We need to sleep. My head is spinning with words.'

******

Dear Mr Monkey,

Last night I believe I was something of a show-off. I believe I was rather horrible to you. I was full of myself and ranting on about what I thought about the novel-as-a-genre and what I thought everything was about.

Really, after a few hours' sleep I woke quite cross with myself. Cross, and ashamed.

I am emailing this to you, by way of an apology.

I am afraid that, during these little nocturnal chats of ours, I have let my hands run on ahead of me and type just what they will. Really, that is no excuse. I've been something of a braggard. Last night I was telling you, I believe, that the lot of us on this godforsaken ship – all we finks and nancies – can interfere with the lives of those of you still living.

I must have been drunk with power. I was ranting. It was most unfair. I should simply be pleased that the two of us have this connection and can talk as we do. I value that and (dare I call it this?) our budding friendship a great deal. It means an awful lot to me, Mr Monkey. You have no idea what it is like to be stuck here with a whole lot of novelists. Many of whom think a great deal of themselves. It makes conversation here quite dull sometimes. Full of hypotheticals.

I try to tell them: It's novel-writing! It's not brain surgery! It's not making rocket ships to fly to Mars! We aren't inventing cures for cancer or AIDS! We're writing fiction and in all honesty, it is supposed to be for fun! Not ours, but for others!

But they give me some terrible scowls and tut-tuttings when I say things like this. I believe my colleagues may think that fun is a trivial thing and a thoughtless thing.

They have to beat their heads and browbeat each other, in order to convince themselves that what they are doing is important, worthwhile, true.

A very sad state of affairs.

Quite a sombre, snappish crew.

No matter.

If the others knew I had this connection with you, and this link to the real world that some of us miss so vitally ... I am sure they would be madly jealous. Why, they might even wrest my laptop off me. I could be quite overpowered by the nancies and finks.

I was never really one for fighting.

Anyway, the point was this: thank you for being my friend.

Another thing, that I thought you ought to be told about. I'm breaking the rules here. Never mind.

Your wife must go to her GP. Those cramps are too regular and severe. She never told you, but when she went to her optician last autumn, he took one look into her eyes and told her she ought to see her doctor. I can't tell you any more about that.

As I tried to explain, Mr Monkey. There are bad things afoot.

Good things, too.

Now, we don't cause them. Don't blame them on me.

I can just give forewarning, for weathering the storm.

The storm here increases its pitch every night.

We are sailing into something frightfully violent and black.

I do hope our vessel can stand it.

With fondest regards,
Iris.

The Tony Story

Glenda had been a star.

He would have to find some way of thanking her.

That was just one more thing to add to the list of things to do now. It was a great long list. There was so much to do and to organise.

Tony woke up in Glenda and Robin's prettily patterned back bedroom and he lay still, faced caked in sleep grit, dried tears, with his mind ticking over all the things that had to be done.

Marion had become a list of things to be ticked off.

Everything had changed. He wasn't even in his own bed. This wasn't just the confused aftermath of some raucous night out. This was it now: his whole life shook about, rearranged, altered forever.

He was lying in a fresh clean bed under a pink and green patterned duvet, by a bookcase filled with paperback novels. It was a room he'd never even seen before.

Now he felt that he'd never see his own bedroom, his own house, ever again. He'd been shaken right out of the orbit of his own life. And he'd never see Marion again, either.

It was almost midday. Automatically he'd reached for his mobile to check the time, before remembering that he'd smashed it in the car park of the hospital after their visit to the morgue. He'd ground it under the heel of his shoe on the gravel. He'd never use one of those things again. With grim pleasure he'd watched its green light disappear.

The sunlight was coming in gentle through the curtains that matched the duvet cover. It was mild and still a little snowy and just the thought of that softness and cold made him sag back down and not want to get up.

But the metal alarm clock on the bookcase said it was almost twelve. He would have to get up and face his rescuers. He would have to make a start on all the work to be done. Maybe Glenda would help him. Maybe she would help him even more.

He had a confused memory of sitting in their front room, at maybe six this morning, with a brandy glass big as a fishbowl. It was warm and fingerprinted in his cupped hands.

That Robin, Glenda's fella, was working on the wood burning stove, trying to warm the house through at an ungodly hour on a wintry morning. All Tony could do was apologise again and again, for disturbing them and ruining their night.

'I've been up all night anyway,' said Robin bluffly. He glanced at Glenda. 'Waiting up for this one, seeing that she was all right.'

Glenda shot her husband an angry look, a chastening look, and Robin had blushed at his mistake.

Then Tony was crying again, shaking out deep, hiccough-ing sobs. Glenda perched herself on the arm of the settee, putting her arms around his shoulders. Tony cried in a resentful way. It was as if he was trying to make each sound that came out of him the last one. As if it embarrassed him. But there was always one more coming up and it fright-ened him, that it wouldn't stop.

Glenda knew that this was just shock. It was just the instant bodily reaction to the night; to seeing all the official paraphenalia of a death. This was the visceral reaction to seeing his wife on that shiny slab under the blue sheet. The real grief was yet to come.

The brandy glass had slipped out of his fingers and spilled over the rug.

Tony started apologising again, bubbles coming out of his nose and mouth as he grabbed after the glass.

*****

Last Night

It was almost last orders.

'Go on, Tony. Try her again.'

'Yeah, go on. Give her another go. See where she is.'

'She'd better get a move on. Shall I get her a drink in? What is it? Gin and Slimline?'

'Yeah. That's what she has.'

The barrel-chested man sighed, feeling got at. He was still in his shirt and tie from work. He felt around in his leather jacket for his mobile.

OK. So he'd try her again. See where she was.

Last time he'd phoned Marion she wasn't even out of London. Telling him she was watching the fuel gauge and how a single mile through Tottenham had taken almost half a tank of petrol. She'd stopped and filled up again and phoned him from the garage.

He could just see her, standing at the till, talking and fiddling with her credit cards.

Everything was more expensive in London anyway. It was no surprise to him that she'd used petrol so quickly, inching along in Friday night traffic.

But it was annoying that she wasn't here yet.

It was him alone amongst all her work mates. All of them steaming and over-friendly with each other. Trying to bring him into it all, pretending they were best mates with him as well. When, really, it was Marion who was in with them all. They wouldn't give tuppence ha'penny for him on his own.

No, he was glad he didn't live in London and he was glad he didn't work with this lot, either. He just wished Marion would hurry up and get here. They could have their little drink. Toast that Glenda goodbye and good luck in her new job, and get off home.

That's all Tony wanted to do.

A noodle bar, for god's sake. Who wanted a noodle bar in Norfolk?

It was too young and trendy a place for Marion's work mates. This crowd of fortysomethings in their sleeveless shirts, chinos, their bra tops on slack flesh and their patterned leggings. Look at that Joyce, coming back from the bar with armfuls of Bacardi Breezers. And Marion said she put on such airs at work in the shop: a manager. Well, if Tony had seen her out by herself, he knew what he'd call her.

'Connecting Marion...' his phone told him, so he watched the little line crawl over the LCD and held it up to his ear in preparation, cupping the other one with his hand.

It was deafening in the noodle bar. All of Marion's work-mates were shouting across the long table at each other, clattering their glasses and bottles and the music was blaring out of the jukebox. Some duh-duh-duh dance kind of thing that just showed what young kind of crowd the noodle bar management really wanted in there, kicking up a storm and handing over their cash on a Friday night.

And it wasn't them. It isn't us, Tony thought, as his phone started to crackle and he squinched up his eyes to concentrate and to listen.

'Marion?' he said, and realised he was shouting. 'Marion?' he tried, more quietly, trying not to sound harassed.

Around him, Marion's workmates had noticed he'd got through, that his shoulders were hunched up and he was straining to listen.

That ginger Geoff was slapping him on the shoulder and yelling at him again: 'Go on, Tony. Tell her to get her arse down here. She's missing all the fun.'

The other end of the line sounded like a bad radio play. Under all the noodle bar noise and the crackles from the line, he could hear the motorway and the car itself. He could even hear Radio Two going. 'Baker Street' by Gerry Rafferty, it sounded like.

'Tony!' Marion was shouting. She always held the thing too close to her mouth. 'I'm still thirty miles away!'

'What are you doing?' he said. 'You must be crawling along!'

'Are you all having a nice time?' she asked. 'Oh, give Glenda my love. Did you give her the card? I don't know if I'll make it. She'll be mad if I miss her!'

On Tony's other side, that big girl, Kim, was looking at him, really close up, as if she was trying to listen in too. 'Is she here yet?' Kim shouted. 'Shush everyone,' she barked down the table. 'Marion's almost here!'

Some of them listened, most of them didn't.

Tony glanced along and Glenda was adjusting her bra strap and talking to some younger bloke.

'What?' Tony said. 'You're breaking up.'

'How long have I got till last orders?'

He turned to ginger Geoff. 'How long at the bar?'

Geoff frowned, comparing the clock above the optics with his own flashy watch. 'About six minutes, I reckon. Shall I get her one then? Where is she? Is she in town yet?'

Tony scowled. 'Course not. Yeah, get her one in.'

He watched ginger Geoff ease himself off the cramped banquette and past all his workmates. Then he hissed into his phone: 'You've put me in a right position this evening. Leaving me with this lot.'

Marion laughed at him. 'Oh, it gets you out of the house.'

'They're awful,' he said. 'How can you put up with them?'

'They're all right,' she said defensively.

'Huh. Anyway. That ginger Geoff's getting you a drink.'

'Bless him.'

Someone was shouting out. It was Kim, beside him, struggling to her feet. 'Everybody!' she announced. She trod on one of Tony's feet and he cursed. 'Everybody!' she yelled and banged her emptied Frascati bottle on the table. 'Attention! I've got a few words to say about Glenda, who's leaving us tonight...'

'What's going on?' Marion asked.

Half the table still weren't listening.

'That Kim's giving a speech.'

'I'm missing it all,' she moaned. 'How were the noodles?'

54

'Bloody awful.'

'Everybody!' Kim screamed.

'Look,' said Marion. 'I'm going to put my foot right down. So I get there before they chuck you all out.'

Now the others were laughing at Kim, who was red in the face and cross because they weren't listening properly.

'Yeah,' Tony said. 'I don't know why you didn't get a shift on earlier. Or set off earlier...'

'I was shopping,' Marion said. 'And you know I can't be hurried. You know that. Look, the traffic's loosening up. I should be okay.'

Ginger Geoff was coming back from the bar, his fingers stretched round pints of bitter, with Marion's small gin at the front.

'I think,' Kim shouted, 'that we should all sing to Glenda, because she's leaving us and because you all obviously don't want to hear me give a speech...'

Raucous cries of approval at this, and thumping of glasses on formica. Kim started up: 'For she's a jolly good fellow...'

And the rest joined in raggedly.

'They're singing along now,' Tony shouted, shaking his head.

'Never mind,' Marion laughed.

Then it was hard to hear her with all the carry-on.

'Look,' she was saying, right in his ear, when he could make her out again. 'I'm really flooring it. I'm flying along. You'd be proud of me...'

The workmates were doing the 'so say all of us' bit. The song was falling apart, breaking up into whoops of laughter. They went onto the cheers, clinking glasses and grinning at Glenda, who was embarrassed, smiling and misty-eyed, all at the same time.

'What?' Tony said, pressing the tiny phone hard to his ear, so hard it made the cartilige crick and twinge with pain.

'I said,' Marion laughed, 'that I'm flying along...'

The workmates finished their hurrays and they started to clap and call out 'Speech! Speech!' And Glenda was waving her hands in front of her face and laughing.

'You're doing what?' Tony yelled.

The engine noise was louder. The line was crackling worse.

Glenda had been dragged to her feet and she was thanking people.

'There's just one thing I want to say to you lot. You who've been such a good team to me, for such a long time...' Glenda was beaming and looking round at them all.

Marion said, 'Tell them I'll be there in about three minutes flat!'

Tony said, 'Marion...'

Then the noise burst out in his eardrum: a huge roar that crushed itself inside his skull. He thought it was the line giving up completely. But it went on for a few seconds – three, four. A horrible drawn out crescendo during which his heart seemed to stop and his mouth dropped open.

Over it all, over all the mechanical noise and static, there was still a human noise. There was still something in it that he recognised.

The phone went dead.

Glenda slurred her words only slightly as she said: 'All I want to say to you is let's carry on boozing and get piss-arsed drunk!'

Her work mates howled with laughter and gave her thunderous applause. Glenda was known to be quite staid at work and they were glad to see her showing another side.

The clapping subsided and Glenda sat down gratefully and they all set about their last drinks. Talk was turning to where they would go next and whether they wanted to brave a club. The night shouldn't end like this, not so soon. Not just because this place was closing.

Tony had taken the phone away from his ear and was staring at the display. It was lit up green and just showing the time now. Nothing seemed to have gone wrong with it.

Ginger Geoff slid the gin and Slimline tonic over to him. 'Here's her drink,' he said. 'Though I reckon someone will have that, if she doesn't show her face.'

'Cheers,' said Tony.

'No problem,' said ginger Geoff.

'Did you lose your connection?' asked Kim, turning to him.

'Uh, yes,' Tony said thickly. 'I think I did.'

His ears were still ringing inside.

******

Now they were going to a club. The decision had been taken and it was Glenda who was egging them on, who said that she'd got her second wind.

They were going to that club in Tombland, the one with the statues propped up in the doorway.

'The one where there's always sick on the pavement outside?' Kim asked.

'Oh, come on,' said Glenda. 'Before we all get too old to go to those kind of places at all.'

Tony left them to go to the toilet as they were pulling on their coats.

They were the last ones in there. The people behind the bar looked impatient.

'Hey, we should go down that lapdancing club.' Ginger Geoff patted his back as he went by. 'What do you think, eh?

Have you seen that advertised? We should take them all down there and give them a shock. Would your Marion go, Tony? Eh? Would she go to a lapdancing joint?'

Tony shouldered past a bit roughly, to find the toilets, staggering slightly on the black and white lino squares.

'Hang on for Tony,' he heard Geoff tell them all. 'I think he's feeling a bit worse for wear...'

The toilets didn't smell very nice. That was the thing with these places that thought they were trendy. It was all just surface gloss.

He went straight to the line of basins and splashed cold water over his face.

It was true. He felt a bit out of it now.

He couldn't be sure of what he'd heard at all.

He looked at his own reflection and his face was blotchy, his eyes a bit red. His hair was standing up in short tufts. A wreck.

He wiped his hands quickly on his trousers and tried Marion's number again, holding in a deep breath.

A flat dull tone came back at him. And the battery wasn't run down. There was nothing wrong with it, far as he could see.

Maybe she'd switched hers off, so she'd be without distractions as she concentrated on her driving and screamed into town.

Maybe she'd be arriving in a flurry at the noodle bar, breathless and all of a whirl, making her work mates laugh, just as Tony came out of the toilet.

And she'd call him over and peck him on the cheek and tell them all that of course she and Tony were coming out to that club.

That's what she'd raced here for. That's what she'd risked life and limb to do tonight.

****

When he came out into the bar again, most of the others had gone and the bar maid was unplugging the jukebox.

Ginger Geoff was waiting in the open door.

'Hey, they've all gone up the road to get in the queue for that club. You coming?'

Tony saw Kim waiting out in the street, hugging herself in her fleece and blowing out smoke.

'I don't think so, Geoff...'

'Oh, come on. You've got your phone. Marion will ring and you can tell her where the party's gone onto...' Geoff ushered him outside, into the chilly, breezy street. 'She'll catch up.'

Nude Disaster Movies

Another car is breaking the speed limit on the same dark road into town. Past two o'clock and there's snow beginning to drift over the forest and the smooth fields. The car throws out its headlights and they flare against the evergreens: the same deep green as bottle after bottle of Gordons gin. John keeps his foot down.

He and Darren are coming back from London. Now they are most of the way home. At the last moment they decided not to sleep on Sandra's floor. They left her flat in Putney and hightailed it back to Norfolk in John's trusty Ka. They have rolled down their windows and David Arnold's CD of Bond themes is playing. The two of them are singing along with 'Diamonds are Forever' and their voices are booming out. But they're speeding and someone standing still in the cramped and gloomy expanses of the woods would never be able to recognise the song. They wouldn't even guess that it was a song. They would just hear shouting as the car roars by. One streak of noise that bursts through the winter woods, leaving nothing behind.

'We really didn't have to be back for tomorrow morning,' Darren breaks off from singing to complain. 'Neither of us have to be at work.' He is thin-faced, peevish; his blond, almost white hair twisted up with wax.

John ignores this for a while, keeping his eyes on the road, staring past the motes of snow swirling in the headlights.

Recklessly Darren carries on. 'Sandra really wanted us to

stay. I think she was keen on the company. I would be, in a big flat like that. She was saying we could have gone out tomorrow, all together. Look at the Tate Modern or something.'

'Oh, yeah,' John says. He has this deep, brown voice too old for him. He doesn't have to raise it over the sound of the motor or the CD. 'Well, I wanted to get back. I didn't want to sleep on her floor. I want my own bed.'

The truth is, John has had about as much as he can take of Sandra. Wanking on about how fantastic it is to live in London. Sandra who takes speed just to get on the Tube to go out to an Irish pub for a couple of hours, and who has to be virtually carried back to that flat of hers. John doesn't know why he let Darren talk him into driving down to London for a night out with her.

Yes he does. Cabin fever in Norfolk.

'Sandra's a great mate,' Darren is saying. 'I'm glad we've all kept in touch since she moved away. And she might be able to get me some freelance work, too, she reckons.' Darren shifts in his seat and flicks his fag butt out of the window. It sticks to the pane on the outside, fizzing slowly in the cold and wet. 'We should have slept on her floor. We needn't have left.'

John casts a sidelong glance at him.

He knows what this business is about. He knows what the whole sleeping-on-the-floor business is about. He knows exactly why Darren was so keen on it tonight. Why camping out and mucking in was right up his street and on the cards tonight.

Once Sandra was away in her tiny bedroom amongst her ethnic artefacts and her bloody dreamcatchers and all that shite, he and Darren would have been all cosied up on her living room floor on a futon under a thin duvet. Just like last time. And that had been the plan. Obviously. Sandra complicit with Darren. Darren acting all innocent, cosying up.

Last time they'd had six pints a piece and a bottle of vodka between them after the pubs had shut and Darren had cuddled up under the duck down duvet and John had found himself kissing him back. Next thing they'd both known, they were tossing each other off on Sandra's Habitat settee. They'd never mentioned it since. That had been New Year and now it was March and Darren has obviously been hoping for a rematch. He was hoping that a return to the location would bring the scene up again in both their minds.

John has done everything he can to forget it. It was only when they got into London this afternoon that he realised what Darren was banking on. When Sandra was saying that they might as well stay the night, now that they'd travelled all the way there ... the whole lurid episode came back, full-force, in his head.

Well, no, they didn't have to stay, actually. And John watched how much he was drinking, determined to drive back home before morning. That bloody Sandra was colluding with Darren. They were ganging up on him to get him back on that floor. Squishing him down on the stripped pine, his head thumping, his mind not made up, defences down, thinking what the fuck, what the hell, doing it anyway. John is fuming, the more he thinks about it, racing through the woods, on the last stretch before their town.

'John, stop!' Darren yells. 'Stop the car!'

He's grabbed John's leg suddenly and John slams on the brakes. The Ka skids a little, but the new tyres hold. John whips around in his seat. 'What the fuck are you on about?' He snaps the stereo off. Then he sees what Darren has seen, on his side of the road. Just a little way further back.

'Jesus,' he says, and reverses along the road.

******

A Fiesta has come off the road, straight into the trees. It's smashed into a trunk and it's a write-off by the looks of things. It looks like a crisp packet, crumpled up and chucked into the roadside.

'Jesus Christ,' John says again as Darren opens up his passenger door. The wreckage is dark, undisturbed. Snow has dropped on it, a light coating, like icing sugar sifted onto a posh dessert.

Darren is moving over to it, slowly. When John switches his engine off it's completely silent. He gets out of his Ka. There is a magnetic force on him. Or the opposite of one; a repulsion, keeping him away from following Darren. He doesn't want to go near.

Darren turns and shouts. 'Have you got a torch?'

'What?'

'A torch. There's still someone in there.'

John is slow and the snowflakes against his face are like tiny burns on his skin. 'Yeah...' He goes back to fetch his torch from the boot. He hears Darren saying, 'It's a woman. She's gone through the fucking screen.'

John is fishing about in the boot, under all the accumulated crap. He's thinking: Just shut the fuck up. I don't want to know anything about it. I don't want to hear about it.

'Come on,' Darren yells.

John forces himself onto the frozen verge, to come and see.

'The door's all fucking buckled up on this side,' Darren says. He's yanking and hauling at it. There's a sharp smell. A horrible smell.

John is staring at the smashed screen, the dark shape slumped over the bonnet, the bright bits of glass scattered everywhere in the snow. There is blood coating the glass and metal, dark and thick, like oil. Smelling like oil, too.

'Your phone,' Darren says shakily, taking the rubberized torch. 'Is your phone charged?'

John is putting a cigarette up to his lips and fiddling with his lighter. He can't get it to catch. Darren sees what he's doing and smacks his hands away, hard, knocking the fag and lighter through the air. The clipper skitters over the car's crumpled roof. 'You can't fucking smoke, you twat!' he screams. 'You'll blow us sky bloody high!'

'Fuck,' John says, shaking his head.

Darren grapples with the torch's buttons and realises they are both talking like people in a film. The beam clicks on. Too dim. He plays it over the ruined car. This is like a scene from a film. That's why they're talking like this, he thinks. This isn't the kind of thing you see in real life. You aren't supposed to. This is the kind of thing that professional people – like police and paramedics – are paid to see. Just so the likes of you won't have to. It shouldn't be up to us to see it and deal with it, Darren thinks. Not us two stuck out here in the woods. Alone with this.

The snow is coming down thicker.

'Get your phone,' Darren says, keeping his voice steady. 'John. Go and get your phone.'

The beam of yellow light is on the woman's body. She's in a smart fuschia suit and her hair is ash blonde. He can't see all of her face. Darren stays there, playing the beam over her and he listens to the distant bleeping of John's phone, and then John gabbling away to someone at a switchboard, trying to give the details.

I have to touch her, Darren thinks. I have to see if there's a pulse. I have to try. Yet he knows there won't be. No matter how badly they get hurt, people don't just lie there in positions like that. Not in all that broken glass and not in all the snow. There's no knowing how long she's been there. Not yet.

He will have to touch a dead woman's skin. It's up to him to see what hope she has.

John is coming up behind. John is calmer now that he's been able to do something practical, businesslike. He comes up just as Darren is touching her wrist with the tips of his fingers. John watches as Darren closes his eyes and bites down hard on his lip and strains his ears.

******

It isn't long until the whole stretch of road in the middle of the woods is filled with vehicles. They've made John move his Ka and the air is flashy and noisy with sirens and people in heavy coats and gloves, dashing about. The stretch of road is thick and lurid with their activity and John and Darren are forced back, away from the scene of the crash. They are being talked at by experts, who want to know details and more details. Times, exact times and events. They want to know the exact extent of their involvement.

What have they done? What have they seen?

Meanwhile other experts are at work on the Fiesta. Darren watches them cutting into the metal, sending up showers of blue sparks. He watches them swarming over the body of the woman. The back of the ambulance is open and it gives out a chilled, pale light, like a fridge. They're hoisting her onto a stretcher. It seems to take hours. They're loading her in.

As John and Darren answer their questions, they look stunned and bewildered by it all, as everything gets taken out of their hands. Only moments ago it was their property, this accident, this wreckage. The road was silent and the car and the body were still warm. Finders keepers. Darren finds himself feeling curiously resentful of the new activity and the busywork around them. Now there's nothing for them to do but answer simple questions.

Not John, though. He looks relieved that this army of helpers has turned up. He looks keen for his own part to be finished and over with. He's dying to get away.

For the first time it strikes Darren that, by rights, it should have been John's job to touch the dead woman's skin, to check for her pulse and find it wasn't there. John's a vet. It would have been easy for him.

'They think we caused it,' John says to Darren, when they're left alone for a moment. 'That's what all the questions are about. They don't believe us, that we just found her, after the crash ...'

Darren looks at him. 'Course they believe us. It's just routine.' He looks up at the snow coming down, sifting through the overhanging branches; the network of stiff, bristled branches against the powdery sky. He tries to imagine how it must have felt to be the woman in the car. He wonders how much she would have been aware of what was happening to her.

They watch the ambulance leave.

Now the wrecked car itself is the focus of the experts' attention and their activity, as if it's just as important as the woman. The policeman who has already questioned them is back. John is asking when they can go. Darren is watching another police car arrive at the edge of the disaster area. He watches more police leading out two very ordinary-looking people. A man and a woman. He is in a shirt. She'll be freezing in that top and skirt. They aren't allowed too near the scene, either. They are allowed to look from a distance, like visiting dignitaries. They are being talked at, briefed.

All too soon it's time for John and Darren to be sent home.

When John starts the car his CD player bursts into life again. It's still on the same track, 'Diamonds are Forever'. Unlike men, the diamonds linger. It comes on too loud and savagely: John switches it off again. He pulls the car away and the road in front is perfect with snow.

That's no blessing on us at all, Darren thinks. That's no consoling benediction. That's just snow: late in March, late at night, still coming down.

It's just random bad weather.

Means nothing at all.

*****

John and Darren stop off at the garage on the main road by the row of shops. They need cigarettes. And chocolate, Darren decides. He needs a rush of blood sugar to calm him down.

They both live in their own, separate houses on a street just down from here. Now they're at the garage they're almost home. They have passed the last few miles to town in silence. They haven't tried to talk about what they've seen.

As they cross the lit forecourt, Darren says, 'We'll have to go down to the police station together, tomorrow morning. I'm not going by myself.'

John nods quickly. The policeman made them an appointment. Just another few questions. A final statement. John doesn't want to talk about it now. They walk into the garage shop and choose handfuls of chocolate bars, crisps, pasties and sidle up to the counter with its plastic barrier. The girl behind the till is very young, Darren thinks, to be up all night like this.

He looks at himself and John, as they appear on the blue CCTV camera, shot from above. As he hands over his stash of goods and asks for his fags he can't help thinking: We do look good together. Even on a security camera. John is looking the other way. Then, while Darren is waiting for John to be served, the shop door bleeps again and someone else is coming in, bleary-eyed and sleepless.

'Robin!' Darren calls the older man over. He's glad to see a familiar face. Seeing Robin here, a neighbour and a work colleague, makes him feel like he's in the right place. The correct dimension. He hasn't, after all, arrived with John in some alternate world where terrible things go on all the time and ordinary members of the public have to deal with warm corpses.

That very phrase makes him feel queasy. 'Warm corpses' sounds sickly and wrong. It makes him feel just like he does when he sees 'warm salmon salad' on a menu. It's like a description of something not quite dead.

Robin looks surprised – and almost shifty – seeing his colleague in the garage shop. 'You're up early,' he says and his voice is rough with smoke. He peers into Darren's face and sees immediately that something is wrong.

'We've just got back from London,' Darren says. 'You wouldn't believe the night we've had.' John has finished now and is looking the newcomer in his denim shirt and tan leather waistcoat up and down suspiciously.

'A hard night out on the town?' Robin laughs.

'We saw a car accident,' Darren blurts. 'Well, the aftermath of one. We found the wreckage. Dead woman lying there.'

Robin's pink eyes go wide. 'No...'

Darren nods and notices that John is looking impatient. He feels ashamed for a moment, as if John is thinking he's relishing the gory details too much.

'We've had to talk to the police and everything.'

'Christ, that's awful,' Robin says. He looks at them both.

'Oh, Robin,' said Darren. 'This is John. A friend from down the street. He's a vet.' The two of them shake hands and Darren is thinking, why am I telling him he's a vet? What's that got to do with it? He says to John, 'Robin lectures in the same department as me.'

'Oh. Right,' says John, not in the least bit interested.

'Are you both okay, then?' Robin asks, kindly. 'I think we've got some brandy in, or something...'

Darren smiles. 'I think we'd better just go home. Call it a night.'

'What a night,' Robin says. 'All that snow came as a shock. I've been working all night. Writing. I didn't know the weather was so bad till I stepped out to buy cigarettes ... And Glenda, my wife ... she's still out there somewhere. Work's night out.'

'I hope she's all right...' says Darren vaguely.

'Oh, she will be.' Robin smiles ruefully and turns to the cash desk. They say their goodbyes and John and Darren step back out into the snow, the bone-cold of the early morning. John leads the way back to his Ka, to drive them the few yards home to their street.

******

There's only one parking spot on their long, quiet street, almost exactly between their houses. They get out and stretch themselves all over again. They listen to the wood pigeons, the dawn chorus starting up in the back gardens.

'I could make coffee,' Darren suggests.

'Nah,' John says. 'I'd better go home.'

'I'm going to have some anyway.'

John shakes his head. He's giving Darren such an odd, hard look that Darren can't help but feel confused.

'Have I done something wrong, John?' he asks. 'I mean, have I pissed you off or something?'

John cricks his neck back and rubs it with his palm. He fiddles with his keys and thoughtfully locks his Ka.

'No,' he says. 'It's okay. I just want to get back to my own place.'

'Okay.'

Darren opens his arms slightly as John steps forward for their habitual, chaste hug. Then he turns and hurries across the street, to his own front door. Darren listens for his door going, as if seeing him safely away.

He watches the sky start to lighten and maybe it's just his eyes playing tricks. He can still feel the pressure of John's hug on his body and he is sure that somehow it feels stronger and more needy than usual. He's sure it does.

****

Sometimes it hits Darren that it's ridiculous, that he and John can spend all this time together and not be in love.

These bleached-out, chilly Saturday afternoons, bustling past remainder bookshops, phone shops, and John remarking on the resurgence in street performers. How much he hates mime artists and silver-faced robot people and clowns with gawking crowds gathered around them. All the mums and dads with kiddies on Saturday, the conspicuous students, white kids with dreadlocks, and the pigeons wheeling around the market stalls like fearless little rats.

We're just filling in time together, Darren thinks.

If John had a girlfriend, or if I had some fella, we'd be spending time with them and we wouldn't be thrown together like this. As it is, we're doing the record shops and bookshops and looking at shoes. We're privvy to each other's most intimate purchases, but only by default. He asks me what I think of this t-shirt, these trainers, can I suggest a third film to buy in his three-for-twenty pounds offer in HMV. He's after my opinions, but I'm only a stand-in. Yet I must be content to do it.

They have things in common, like films. They both like disaster movies of the Seventies, horror movies of the Sixties. Darren also likes Bette Davis and Joan Crawford in films from the Thirties and John will generally sit through these with him, too. He'll be pointing out things to do with lighting and continuity and he'll tell Darren he's such a clichéd faggot.

They're both fans of twentieth century tat. All the things left over and reduced in price.

Every Saturday tea time they end up at Darren's house for cocktail hour. They pop on some retro lounge-core CD and drink vodka with cranberry juice out of tall glasses, sometimes with umbrellas stuck in, planning out the night ahead.

With his sketchy memory of school natural history, Darren firmly believes in the slow, steady progress, the evolution, of love. With his rather better memory for the novels he teaches at the university, he believes, like a nineteenth century heroine, that people can fall into love quite gently. Grafting their however-disparate desires together. He believes in erosion and deposition of affections as surely as rivers do.

He thinks all this investment of time must mean something.

Every four o'clock in the morning, watching Mildred Pierce again, every Bank Holiday Monday with *The Towering Inferno*, with Spanish Cava mixed with sweet peach schnapps ... it must a step towards something. A life spent with someone.

But John is diffident.

He comes knocking on Darren's front door shouting: 'Open up, faggot.' He comes bouncing into the house and he'll be acting like he could be doing anything, seeing anyone. It's just by chance that it happens to be Darren every time.

Darren flinches whenever John talks about some girl he's met. It always seems like such a put-on thing, something done just so he can brag about it. But Darren thinks he knows better. He remembers all too clearly what happened on New Year's Eve, on Sandra's Habitat sofa. Even if, in some subtle, underhand manner, John has made it clear that he doesn't want to discuss it further.

Darren is glancing at him now, as they walk through the covered market place. Here, all the stalls seem wonky and they spread in a ramshackle fashion up a gentle incline, so Darren feels that his balance is shot because there are no straight lines and he ends up having to shove his way through all the gawkers and the air reeks of frying bacon, sausage, coffee and local cheese. He watches John pushing ahead in his brown suede jacket and his jeans where the seams twist round on the knee. And Darren can hardly credit that once – for one night only! – he saw his straight friend with nothing on.

His everso straight, dyed-in-the-wool, protesting-too-much pal, showing off his flat, lightly-tanned stomach with its whirlpool of glossy black hair. And John was in command that time, of course, delivering firm instruction on how he wanted his cock sucked. Darren was keen to display his expertise: his tongue teasing under the head of John's cock, holding him back as far as he'd go, tickling up the length of the shaft with his lips, taking John's balls whole into his mouth.

John said, 'So I'm gay! I'm gay after all. After everything.' It was one of the few things he said at all that night. He sprang off the settee and danced around in the dark, scattered living room and Darren watched him, wanting to laugh. He wanted to laugh at John's sprightly silhouette, his ridiculously long, still hard dick bobbing about. John was dancing around like a boxer. He was shadow-boxing as he asked: 'Am I gay? Is that it now?'

Then he came back to lie right on top of Darren, kissing him again – exasperated, astonished kisses – pulling away each time to look down at him, making them both laugh now.

'It's just like being little boys,' he said, later the next day, when the two of them slouched round Spitalfields market, hungover, looking at old books and board games and having chilli for lunch. 'It's like being little boys, playing with each other...'

Darren knew he looked incredulous. 'I never played like that when I was a kid!'

John shrugged and pulled a face. And he hasn't mentioned their adventure since, not once in the three months since.

Sometimes Darren thinks about something John said, when they woke together, clasped up, naked, sweating in the morning. 'You're not really like a gay man. You're like a straight man and a straight woman, both at the same time.'

Darren has puzzled over that. Was John trying to get out of it somehow? Excusing himself for how much he'd been into it? But he didn't dwell on this as much as he did the remembered image of John stripping himself down in the half-light – all matter of factly – as if he was changing in the gym or the swimming baths.

Darren needs to shake himself out of this. He needs to get into a conversation with John about something that isn't sex. They end up looking at lamps in Habitat and then they're getting a pint in a cafe bar decked out in blonde wood, grey settees, beanbags.

******

They take the settees by the fire, just as two people are leaving. Two pretty miserable-looking middle-aged people.

'Did you see the two of them!' John laughs, after a first swig of his fizzy Kronenburg. 'I'd hate to get to that age and look

like them ...' He goes on, with a casual kind of dismissive-
ness and bitchiness that Darren doesn't really like when it
comes out in his friend. 'They looked really pissed off to
be out together. Like they'd just been thrown together and
there was no point in it ... no joy in it.' John shakes his
head. 'And as if they hate their work and all their lives, too.
Jesus, if I get like that I'll be straight in the medicine cabinet at work. I'll dose myself up and hello darkness my old
friend.'

'You wouldn't!' Darren says.

John nods.

'Anyway,' Darren says, 'Would animal medicines work on
human beings?'

'Of course. It's all the same stuff. It's made by the same
companies. Just weaker doses.'

Darren thinks. 'Yeah, but ... dog chocolate is different to
human chocolate, isn't it? And so are dog biscuits ... they're
different, too ...'

John shakes his head. 'You're fucking daft, Daz.'

'Yup.'

'Anyway,' John says. 'I don't reckon that woman was as old
as she looked, do you? I bet she was our age. The bloke was
older. She was just one of them who look older because
their lives are so fucked-up and thwarted.'

Darren can't help laughing at him. 'That's charitable of you.'

'I mean it, though,' says John. 'Our lives are great, aren't they? I mean, we've only got ourselves to please. To look after. We'll never look all careworn like them two sat here did. They were probably married to each other.'

'Or they were having an affair,' Darren says.

'A bloody miserable one. Imagine that – a miserable affair.' John hefts his pint again. Suddenly it's only half full. 'And now they're back off to their miserable jobs. In some bloody horrible shop, by the looks of it. Soulless.' He looks straight at Darren, which surprises them both. It's not often that John looks him in the eye these days. 'Imagine doing something you didn't want to do.'

Something curdles in Darren's stomach at this and he feels like bursting out that he loathes what he does. He hates every minute of it. That when he gets to work each morning and before every class he teaches, he makes himself throw up.

'What we've got,' says John, 'is vocations.'

'Sick animals and spoiled students,' Darren says.

'Hm,' John sniffs. 'I wish they were sicker. People bring these perfectly happy animals into the surgery and I'm reduced to stupid things like weighing dogs and cats and taking their temperatures. There's some funny people taking animals to surgeries. It's like Munchausen's by proxy. They bring their pets in for things they'd never dream of going to the doctors for themselves.'

'People don't look after themselves,' says Darren vaguely. But neither do I, he thinks.

****

This Saturday Cocktail Hour goes on all night.

It's the usual thing. If they don't fix on something in particular to do, Darren and John carry on drinking and the next thing they know it's two in the morning. They've always got such a lot to say to each other. This Saturday there's nothing on at the pictures and they don't fancy any club or bar. Or rather, Darren wouldn't have minded going out somewhere queer, but didn't want to suggest it. They wind up in Darren's half-painted living room, watching *Earthquake*, which John bought this afternoon.

'It's going to be one of those nights where we watch film after film all night,' John says, 'and they end up making less and less sense as it goes on ...'

Darren keeps doing that thing with the time, saying: 'This time yesterday...' and dutifully logging everything that went on then. John can't see the point in it. He knows Darren is waiting, counting down for the exact moment when they found the body.

'Marion,' Darren's now calling the body, as if they knew her. The police told them the name this morning, during their quick, almost brusque visit to the police station. Darren keeps calling her Marion and he's made her into an acquaintance, drawing her into the conversation only to dispel her again. They're both being rather heartless about Marion, pouring an extra drink for her and toasting her memory, conjuring the little they know of her. Gradually the joke wears off and they try not to mention her again.

But she's there. At one point Darren says that he wants to go to the corner shop to fetch the local paper, see if there's anything in there about her. John tells him not to be so morbid.

Blearily Darren asks John, 'How come you love disaster movies so much?' He's asked him this before, of course he has.

John shrugs. 'I like knowing, right at the offset, out of all these characters, who's going to live and who's going to die. I like knowing that, at the end, whatever they go through, it's going to be okay.'

'That only works if you've seen it before.'

'That's why I've watched them again and again,' John says. The copy of *Earthquake* he bought this afternoon is to replace his old, worn out one.

'So you don't like new disaster movies?'

'Hate them.' John looks at Darren and smiles. 'Anyway, they don't really make new disaster movies any more.'

'Yes, they do. They had a resurgence.'

'Not proper ones with ensemble casts and proper movie stars. And proper disasters ...'

Darren starts counting off on his fingers. 'Infernos, floods, volcanoes, earthquakes, asteroids, meteors ...' He laughs. 'Giant sharks, killer whales, colossal spiders and mutant bees ...'

John sighs. 'They don't count.' He concentrates on the screen. 'Look, Ava Gardner's coming back on, drunk. You should like this bit.'

'It's all about the sublime, isn't it?' Darren says, some moments later.

John raises his eyebrows.

'Disaster movies. They're all about something bigger than people are. And they're all thrown together in the face of the sublime ... the force of God ... something unaccountable and wayward ...'

'*The Towering Inferno* wasn't a force of God,' John says. 'That was human error. So was *The Poseidon Adventure*. Hey, you missed that off your list.'

'How could I miss that one?'

'It's the best one.'

'Better than *Titanic*?' Darren laughs.

John punches him in the side, winding him more than he means to.

'You should think so, too,' John says. '*The Poseidon Adventure's* quite faggy in parts. When Shelley Winters drowns, swimming under the bulkhead to save them, after giving her swimming medal to her old husband ... "Kiss our grandchildren for me..."'

'Noble, ghastly deaths by leading ladies,' Darren smiles. 'Is that faggy?'

'Are you kidding?' John shakes his head. 'Sublime. Jesus. You literary wanker.'

'I am. I am.' Darren keeps quiet for a few moments and then he goes on, making John curse and reach for the Absolut, which they're drinking neat by now. It's raw and fumey. 'It's like Spielberg,' Darren says. 'All of his films are about encounters with the Sublime, too. All these little glimpses that build up and build up, until he decides that he can show us ... the unshowable.'

'What are you on about now?'

'Whether it's a big shark or the mother ship in *Close Encounters* ... or, like, dinosaurs brought back to life. He's working to convince us – Look! You can actually see this! This thing that you never thought you would! I'm showing the unshowable!'

'Yeah, yeah,' says John.

'And he's even the same in *Schindler's List*. The way he presents the heap of dead bodies in the camp. That's the same technique he uses, showing that – the unimaginable ... making it real. But it's all just spectacle to him, the way he presents it ... it's just like another big dinosaur or a massive fucking shark jumping out of the sea ...'

John says, 'Well, I like the unshowable, as it happens. I think there should be more of it.'

'What about men's cocks in films? Showing erections on the telly? You don't see them much.'

'Are they sublime, too?' John mocks.

'Yup. Do you want to see more of them?'

'Not really. But they don't show much pussy, either.'

'Yes they do. There's more pussy, as you put it, in films than there is down that surgery of yours.'

'Get away,' John says. 'Hey, wouldn't that be great - a disaster movie about a giant vagina?'

'*Attack of the Fifty Foot Woman*,' Darren says.

'Doesn't count. You don't see anything.'

'At The Earth's Core, with Peter Cushing and Doug MacClure.'

'*At The Earth's Soft Core*. How's that about pussy?'

'They travel to the centre of the world in this metal mole with a corkscrew tip and in there it's all, like, primordial, with all these savage women in the jungle and a pink sky and ...'

'You're such a hopeless Freudian, Darren.'

'Writers are meant to be a bit stupid. It helps.'

John thinks for a bit. 'I suppose *Jaws* is all about a great big pussy.'

'Jesus,' says Darren. 'Can we stop now?'

'Maybe all disaster movies are about pussy,' John says. 'When you think about it, it's the fellas who are forced to deal with all the disaster. Like Charlton Heston and Steve McQueen and Paul Newman. And the women all go out of control. They're causing all this mayhem and dying...'

'So,' says Darren, delighted that John has warmed to his theme. 'You like films that are about women getting out of control, causing chaos and having to be killed?'

'Yeah,' says John. 'That's not too good, is it? What does that say about me?'

Before Darren knows what he's saying, he laughs and tells him, 'No wonder you're all mixed up.'

John flashes a look and opens his mouth to say something, and stops.

'Hey,' says Darren. 'Do you want some coffee now?'

It's past one o'clock. John shrugs. 'If there's no booze left.'

'Just funny-looking liquers from the continent.'

'Have them later. Yeah, I'll have coffee.'

Darren gets up and walks through to the kitchen, leaving John with his film.

******

They're both obscurely glad to be out of the conversation. They always feel a little embarrased if they get too analytical watching films together. A couple of times in the past John has accused Darren of lecturing at him and Darren hates that. He tries to enjoy these films with John for just what they are. Silly extravagant things with horrible stuff happening to people you quite like.

As he waits for the kettle to boil Darren unlocks and unbolts the back door and the seal on the cold air outside breaks with a loud crack.

It's pleasantly cool and pitch black out there. It's inviting. The honeysuckle is madly overgrown on the trellis already and it's crackling in the breeze. The moon lights up the narrow, brick-walled garden only sparsely.

Suddenly Darren is aware of wanting to walk out on his winter-damaged turf in his bare feet. The kettle clicks and he hurriedly fills the cafetiere till it foams, too strong, right up to the top. Then he slips off his trainers and socks and goes padding outside, loving the cold of the stone and then the black, damp mud on the soles of his feet.

It's quiet out here. He stands in the middle of his small lawn and stares up, letting the silhouettes of the leaves and branches resolve themselves against the stark, deep blue of the sky.

Darren thinks about looking up at the same sky last night, through different trees. Last night Darren was at the scene of the accident, with all this fussing and horror about him. And snow! This time last night there *was* been all that snow. Now you'd never know. Now he's got bare feet in the mud. Tonight he's in his own near-silent garden and he can relax.

And I'm still alive, he thinks. I'm still alive.

It's his place, in amongst a whole lot of other narrow gardens. Only a few late lights are still on in the terraced houses out back.

Peaceful night.

He touches the bare, pale bulbs of the camellia and wishes they were out, soaking up the wan light. Carefully he unzips and drops his combat trousers and wriggles out of his shirt and t-shirt. He tosses them onto the garden table and listens to his keys and change clank down on the metal.

Silence again and he slides off his pants, chucking them the same way and he lets his skin absorb the night air, goose bumping him all over. He even lifts his arms up into the air. I'm doing the full DH Lawrence moment, he thinks, and rubs his limbs, as if he really is bathing himself in the darkness, lathering himself in its creamy suds.

John is in the kitchen window then, blinking at the dark, stooped over the sink. 'What about this coffee?' he yells. 'Are you out there, Daz, you fag?'

He can't see me, Darren thinks. I've merged with all the green and the branches. I've effaced myself. 'I'm out here,' he says, just loud enough and calm. 'I just came out for some air.'

'Oh. Right.'

The kitchen light pours out onto the long, bobbing leaves of the honeysuckle. They are such a rich green. The door opens and out comes John, knocking against the 1970s telly that broke last autumn and Darren dumped out back, not sure what to do with it. He's thought vaguely of potting plants in it, having them grow through the screen, but then he worried about having jagged shards of broken glass about the place.

'Jesus, Daz,' John says. 'You keep all sorts of crap out here.'

He's coming up to the trellis, up the step onto the lawn. He's looming in the dark, carrying two coffee mugs, sending scarves of mist into the air. Darren can smell it.

'Where the fuck are you? I brought your coffee. No milk, no sugar.'

Darren reaches out to take his. 'Cheers. I've got to warn you, though. I've stripped off.'

There's a pause while John's eyes adjust to the dark. 'What have you done that for?'

'I don't know. It just seemed the thing to do.'

'You'll freeze your bollocks off, man.'

Darren shrugs and sits down, cross-legged on the damp, sparse grass.

John stares down at him, just about making out the gleam of moon on his hair. And then he can see him, knees crooked, holding his coffee mug in one hand, the other arm supporting him. His dark nipples look like eyes.

'You're a funny fella, Daz.'

'You could light the torches,' Darren says.

John finds his new lighter and does as he's told. The torches are four long tapers stuck in the flower beds.

'If I light you up, all your neighbours are gunna see you, Daz.'

'It doesn't really matter.'

Flames sputter and spurt out of the tall, still-wet candles. Soon the garden is a shifting mass of shadows, thrown hither and thither by the uncertain flames. The candlelight is harsh and then gentle and when they're all lit, John is left with just his coffee to drink and only Darren to look at.

He's made a kind of theatre stage, John thinks. He's forced my attention from the telly indoors and made me look at him naked. Fuck.

But then, Darren is sitting with his knees up, almost demure. It isn't like he's flashing his cock in John's face. Cool down, John, he tells himself.

'You can't stay out here too long, Daz,' he says.

'When I was a kid I used to do this all the time,' Darren says. 'Me and some mates. We'd play in the woods and pretend like we were the only people left in the world and we had to survive. And we always had to survive with no clothes on, for some reason. Come on, John … get your things off.'

John clicks his tongue. 'Um … I don't think I'm going there, Daz.'

'You're the pussy then, John.'

'Fuck off.'

'Scared of the cold.'

'It's not the cold I'm scared of.'

They pause then and drink their coffee.

John relents, feeling that he's been too harsh. The coffee is bitter inside him and he feels more drunk suddenly. He sits on the ground, finding a bit of paving stone so his jeans won't get mucky.

John laughs. 'Look at you, showing off. It's not like I haven't seen it all before, Daz.' He says this quietly. Darren is surprised and pleased. It's an admission, a concesssion.

Darren lies back, full length, contented on the cool, densely packed earth. He feels his cock slap back along his belly, growing harder.

John sets down his coffee cup and there is a whisper of cloth as he hoiks off his t-shirt. 'That's as far as I'm going, mate,' he smiles, sitting cross-legged and bunching the shirt up in his hands.

Darren looks at him, and tries to shrug lying down. 'Hey, do what you want.'

'I will.'

'Good.'

John nods, unconsciously rubbing his chest warm. 'I don't do anything I don't want to.'

Darren's mind is racing. Are they still alluding back to their New Year's Eve adventure? If so, what does John mean by that?

John goes on, 'I do love you, mate. I mean, as a pal. As a mate.'

He lets that settle in. He's a few steps on in the conversation from Darren. 'I mean it. I love you to bits. That's why we knock about together so much. But when we ... did stuff, that was a mistake. It's not really my scene, Daz.'

Darren's mouth has gone dry. 'We haven't really talked about it. I thought we were pretending it hadn't happened.'

John laughs softly. 'I was thinking about it for ages after. And I just felt awful.'

'Was it that bad?'

'It just wasn't for me, Daz. It just didn't feel right.'

All right, Darren thinks. I've heard enough now. You can stop explaining yourself.

But John is saying, 'And what I kept thinking of, was how, after we were fooling about and kissing ... and then suddenly it was serious and we were, you know, getting our pants off and it was obvious to both of us what we were going to do ... It wasn't just messing. I almost died when we did that. Couldn't fucking believe I was taking down my pants for you.'

'Yeah,' said Darren. 'I couldn't believe it either.' It sounds much more doleful than he wants it to.

'What disturbed me was how pleased you were, Daz. Like almost relieved that it was happening. Like you'd been expecting it to for ages and that it was just the fulfilment of something that was bound to happen ...'

Darren is sitting up, braced on one elbow. 'But I was pleased! How was I supposed to react? I couldn't have been blasé about it.'

John is struggling to put his thoughts clearly. 'It was the thinking it was inevitable that upset me afterwards. Like you'd succeeded in tricking me, in changing me ...'

'That's only if you assume seduction is a bad thing,' says Darren. It comes out quickly, maybe too glibly. 'It's not a bad thing, John. I seduced you. You didn't like it much. I wish I'd known at the time.'

'It was like you'd tricked me,' John repeats. 'I've really thought it over for ages. I've hated you sometimes.' John gropes around for his coffee, which is coolling rapidly. 'So there's no point in whipping your clothes off like this.'

'That's not why I was doing it.'

'No?'

'I don't know. I just wanted to be naked. Jesus, John. I'm not the enemy.'

'I shouldn't have talked about it,' John says.

'Well, we know where we stand now, I reckon,' says Darren.

'Yeah,' John is clambering to his feet, twisting his t-shirt into a rope.

'I'll try and put some distance between us,' Darren says. 'If that'll make it easier.'

John hisses out his breath. 'I wish I had, like, really liked it, Daz. In a way – honest – I wish I had ...'

Darren shrugs as John starts to move away. He watches him go inside, and the kitchen light is bright on his long, bare back.

******

Darren follows his pal back indoors.

They look at each other.

'You left your clothes out there,' John says, trying to laugh.

'Don't think I'm putting them back on just for you,' Darren says.

Then he catches John's eye, and John is giving him a look up and down. A long, judicious look up and down. They stand like that for a moment, frozen.

Darren chances his arm. Nothing to lose now, anyway. 'Look how hard your nipples have gone.' He looks John in the face and John grins slowly.

'My dick's hard, too. You fucker. You tricky little fucker.'

Darren can see the outline in his soft jeans as John's hands drop down and start to unfasten them.

'Maybe,' Darren says, 'it's like new disaster movies and you have to watch them more than once to get the hang of them. To see if you really like them.'

He steps closer as John strips his own jeans off, unhooking them from one foot at a time.

'Nude disaster movies?' John asks. 'What are they?'

'I think we're in one,' Darren says.

They hug then, going into one of their usual, last-thing-at-night hugs. That's how it will begin.

'Just once more round the block,' John says. 'And if I'm not into it this time, never again. Okay?'

Darren leans in to kiss him. Just now he'd agree to anything.

'Okay.'

*****

Darren thinks he's been asleep for a while, but he hasn't.

He's been lying in the dark, overstimulated on coffee and fags and booze, a bit of sex, and lying in a fug and the dark, and that's quite enough like sleep to make it count.

But it isn't sleep.

John's asleep next to him. He's breathing slow. Darren can feel that ribcage moving gently, all bone and gentle air and skin, like a balloon going up. It's mechanical, gentle, and it ought to be reassuring. It ought to be calming and making him sleep, too.

Instead, of course, Darren lies with his mind racing, his head all tight and hot on the pillow.

How can he, how can John lie so easy on that other pillow? When it isn't even his? Darren hates that. It makes John seem promiscuous and easy somehow, that he can fall asleep on unfamiliar pillows. Unfair, he knows, but understandable, all the same.

It's past three-thirty and Darren thinks about what to do next, since falling asleep with a pounding head is such an impossibility. Also with limbs jangling and a mouth producing saliva that seems like poison. And if he tastes really hard and thinks about it, thinks about it really hard (because he still doesn't believe it, not in any real sense) that's John he can taste. That's what he's got preserved as evidence, so that in any court of law (say, if taste counted for anything) he could even prove to twelve good men and true that John has come in his mouth at last and ... Jesus, what's he thinking of?

But John has fallen asleep, oh so gladly. He even fell asleep with Darren's cock stuck in his gob. Darren's cock is smarting now. Hurray. You've won, Darren, if a competition it was. That prize is all yours, sticky, unwrapped.

He gets up out of bed and wonders what he can do next. What more mischief he can get up to. He needs to racket about the empty house and do stuff, knowing that he's got his man, the one he's aimed at having, if truth be told, in his bed at last. In his bed at last. He's thinking about phoning his last boyfriend and seeing how he's doing in the early hours. He'll do this in the living room, sitting under the lamp in a pool of golden light, talking quietly, hoarsely, knowing he's got the comfort of his new fella sleeping in his bed and stuck there till mid-morning at least.

It seems mightily tantalising, infinitely exciting. Just doing normal, middle of the night stuff in the house that reeks of fags, the still air ripe with all of last night seems exciting now and novel. Just because John is here. And John has fallen for everything Darren has to offer. And Darren can still hardly believe it. Jesus, he sucked my cock.

I want to slap him awake and ask if we're in love now. If we can actually say that. Did you really suck me off?

But Darren is a grown up and he knows by now how to play it a little bit cooler than that. Fuck it – he still wants to slap John awake. I know you're sweaty and stiff and confused and we're both stuck with stuff and reeking of sex. Just fuck me again and prove it to me. Prove it again, now I'm a bit more sober and it's closer to dawn. I just need to know it's truer than I thought it was.

But John sleeps on. His body is radiating this tremendous

heat. Darren can lie alongside him and clasp him and feel much too hot. He minds, really, that it's quite so hot. It's hot and it's John lying there and still he can't quite take it in.

Soon the birds are starting up an outrageous dawn chorus. He's never thought about how extravagant they are. How they sound. This is every morning. And he's never listened properly.

John sleeps on and he's wonderfully still, apart from that gentle ribcage thing.

If only I could have that ribcage moving so gently all the time. He's so warm he's like Sunday dinner slowly cooking. He's like Sunday dinner already in the middle and the thickest part of Saturday night. He's a roast dinner.

Darren doesn't sleep a wink. He's got all of this going on. He hardly knows where to put himself. Christmas night, Christmas morning. It's as good as all that. John is on a baking tray next to him and Darren can't sleep. He just basks in the oven. He's marvelling, really. Marvelling at his own cooking and the oil, the bread sauce and the flesh falling neat off the bone.

You've got to skewer it and see if the juices run clear. He remembers that much. And that's how you tell that it's done.

Glenda

1

Glenda was sitting at a side table. She was sipping water from a bottle and trying to talk with Kim.

This is my party and I'm drinking water and I'm trying to talk with Kim, she thought. Does it get any better than this? The rough plush of the sofa was harsh against the bare skin of her legs and she was far too hot. She glanced to where the others were dancing and wondered how they could manage it. She was amazed at them, holding their own in this place full of teenagers.

Kim was quizzing her, that was plain. When Glenda could bring herself to even partly concentrate on what Kim was saying, she found that Kim was wanting to know who would get her job, now that she was gone.

She should have known this would happen. As soon as Kim got her on her own.

Glenda hitched her bra strap and said, 'I really don't know what they'll do. Honestly, Kim. And they're cutting down anyway. You know that.'

'Of course I do.'

The company's misfortunes were well known. A famous British department store; once rock solid, now going down the tubes. No one had said it out loud, but that uncertainty was part of the reason Glenda was leaving.

'But they'll still need someone in your job, won't they?'

Glenda just nodded and decided to let Kim think what she wanted. That was the best way, with people like her. If anything, Glenda thought, if anyone should have my position, then it's Marion. Promote Marion off her deli counter. That's what Glenda would have advised. Not that anyone had asked her, though. All the top-level decisions came filtering mysteriously through the ether; communicated by fax, email, phone call. It wasn't as if real people were making any decisions anymore.

Now Kim was banging on about what was wrong with the store's new collections. And how she would improve the store's fortunes and battered reputation.

'It stands to reason. We shouldn't be catering for people who want designer stuff. Clothes that are in this season, out the next. What we are is dependable and sensible. We should keep the styles a bit casual and comfortable, but it should still be quality stuff and a bit smart.' Kim ran her fingers through her fading perm. 'That's what people want, isn't it? Your people in the street. They don't want anything too way-out.'

'Hm,' said Glenda and sipped her bottled water. Time was, she thought, the only people you saw drinking water like this were people on long-distance bike races. Tour-de-France, things like that. Now here she was at forty-six, sipping out of a plastic bottle in a disco. It was all very odd.

She was starting to wish they had stopped the night after the noodle bar. It was her fault. She'd been carried away on too many drinks bought for her, buoyed along by the real affection her colleagues seemed to be showing, and their evident regret at losing her.

Glenda had been made sentimental by the attention and now here she was, watching them trying to keep up with the speed of the music and the flashing lights. And she was being harangued by Kim, who was over-keen and not her favourite work mate.

Also, her noodles were repeating on her.

'I almost died,' Kim was ranting. 'When the new summer stock came in last year. Really, when I first saw them. I took one look and I almost fell over. Tie dye! Tie dye t-shirts and jeans! Well, what was that all about? Everyone dressing like beach bums and hippies. That's not our end of the market.'

'Hm,' said Glenda.

'And those awful underwear adverts with so-called real women posing in our bras and pants. Some of those women were fifty if they were a day. And we've got their pictures blown up twice life-size! I said to Geoff, we'll get all sorts of perverts coming in to see them things. Who wants to see someone with grey hair in nothing but their undies?'

Kim was in her late thirties and she was very loyal to the store. She clearly saw herself working there for life, advancing though the ranks towards the inhouse pension plan and the retired staff association and she wasn't afraid to show it. She had a terrible zeal about her, Glenda thought and she took it very personally when they discussed the rocky fortunes of the store on programmes like *Newsnight*.

'If they only asked me,' Kim was saying. 'I could tell them what we do best. I could tell them what people expect of us. Well, we're holding up a standard, aren't we? For people to aspire to. We show them the way, or we should. I could turn it all around for us. I really think I could. I'd know what to do ... just instinctively...'

Glenda tried to imagine anyone asking Kim for an opinion about anything. They wouldn't need to ask. If she saw someone in the street with a clipboard, she probably approached them first.

Glenda was startled then, because Kim was looking at her oddly. There was a kind of conspiratorial leer on her face. 'You haven't said much about the job you're going on to, Glenda...'

Glenda swallowed and pretended that the music was too fierce.

'I said, what's this great job that you're moving to?'

There was no escaping her.

Glenda found herself scowling at Kim's great big folded up arms. Suddenly she hated her and it was the likes of Kim who were the reason she was leaving her job.

The truth was, there was no fantastic job she was moving to. Everyone had simply assumed there was. The likes of Kim would never credit that, that Glenda would leave such a wonderful world to do precisely nothing.

Kim's mouth was hanging open, waiting for her answer.

Glenda found herself standing up abruptly, and shouldering her bag. 'You know what, Kim?' she shouted. 'You could trap flies in that mouth of yours.'

Kim looked dumbfounded when she realised what Glenda had said. 'What?'

Glenda extricated herself from the table and all the debris.

'I said, Kim, that you're mad if you think you stand a chance at a management job. The whole thing is going down the pan and you are going with it.' Glenda leaned in closer and caught a whiff of her shocked colleague's tangy sweat. 'You are a dull and stupid woman, Kim. You're pushy and you get on everybody's nerves. And, just to satisfy your curiosity, I'll tell you something else. I'm leaving my job to go and do precisely bugger all. I'm going to put my feet up and live off my fella and when I think about you standing about on your fat ankles all day long while I'm lolling about at home, I'll laugh like a fucking drain.'

She put down her water bottle and took one last look at Kim's red face. Then she marched to the bar.

2

They had some special promotion on, where you could get these little shooters in plastic glasses. They were flavoured Schnapps.

Right, that'll do, she thought. Glenda elbowed up to the wet stainless steel of the bar and ordered herself a vanilla shot. It cost nearly four pounds and tasted just like custard. 'Oh. Hi, Tony.'

He was leaning on the bar with his shirt sleeves rolled up. She couldn't help noticing they were soaked through with spilled drink. He nodded to her.

'No Marion, eh?' she asked, and rolled her eyes. 'What did you say she was doing today?'

Waiting for Tony to answer, Glenda stole a glance at herself in the mirror behind the bar. It hadn't misted up too much and she saw that she looked okay. Her short dark hair was in place and her face hadn't gone too red. She looked fine. She looked back at Tony and raised her eyebrows. Jesus, he looked a state. She was surprised at him.

'Marion was in London,' he said. 'Shopping. One of her little trips out by herself.'

'You'd think she'd have got herself back in time,' Glenda said, lifting her shot glass up again and taking the last little dribble. 'It being my big night and all. I thought Marion was my pal.'

Tony was gawping at her. His mouth was going like a goldfish's.

'What?' she asked him.

'The thing is,' he said. 'I think there might have been an accident.'

Now he'd said it, he looked even worse.

'What are you talking about?' But suddenly Glenda had gone cold inside.

'An accident,' he said again, louder.

Glenda looked at her watch. It was almost two.

'Marion?' she asked.

To get any sense out of him she had to drag him back through the foyer and out into the street.

Only when they were out there, by the bouncers and where some young lad was throwing up in the road, did Glenda realise that she'd left her coat and all her leaving presents and cards back in the cloakroom. She'd have to pay to get in again and fetch them, probably.

But her mind was racing anyway in the freezing street and she was trying to make sense of what Tony was on about, grabbing him by both shoulders.

He towered over her like a monstrous, middle-aged child. He had his mobile phone out again, blubbering, offering to show it to her, the screen lighting up. Glenda wondered if all her staff had seen her leaving with him. Knowing that lot, they'd put it about that she was copping off with him. Great. But they were no longer her staff. She'd left now.

The relative quiet of Tombland at two in the morning came as as much of a shock as the cold. The two of them shouted at each other like deaf people.

'I can't get her!' he was moaning. 'I can't get her signal!'

The bouncers were looking over. In their black djs, hands over their crotches like footballers during a penalty shoot-out. Chuckling to each other about the state their punters got themselves into.

Glenda hauled Tony over to a bench outside the antiques shop next door. There was something sinister about all that silver in the window, all that old-fashioned cutlery laid out just so.

She got him to tell her the whole tale.

And as he stammered it out, more of that cold, certain feeling went right through her.

It was colder than two o'clock in the morning in the middle of town. Colder than a mini skirt and strappy top and gooseflesh outside a dingy nightclub.

And she knew, as Tony told the tale and tried to get her to be the sensible one - her, Glenda, being the sensible one; managing as usual - she just knew at that point that Marion was dead.

3

Glenda thought about phoning her husband to explain. But Robin would either be working late, or he'd be asleep. Either way he wouldn't want disturbing with news like this. High drama. He'd be concerned for her and her involvement, but he'd point out reasonably that there was nothing he could do and he'd wonder why she'd disturbed him like that.

So she sat in the back of the police car holding Tony's clammy hand and decided that it could wait till she got back home. Whenever that would be.

She'd sobered up immediately, out on the street in Tombland, as soon as it had become clear what Tony was talking about. When he'd told her about the broken line and the noise he'd heard under all the hullaballoo of the noodle bar, she'd known that his first thoughts had been correct and that Marion had been killed. But by then Tony was trying to talk himself out of it. There'd been no accident. Marion would be fine. She had decided not to come out. She was far too tired and he would find her at home, all safe, just as Glenda would find Robin.

Glenda had taken Tony's phone off him and she'd called the police. Pressing the glowing green buttons firmly and talking with the switchboard woman in a clear, even voice. A professional voice. Somehow, with the bouncers watching and the nightclub-goers starting to filter out onto the pavement around them, she felt the need to sound more sober and controlled than she ever had before.

Tony had gone to pieces. She could tell that much. Why on earth hadn't he said anything sooner? To have heard that noise of his own wife crashing her car and then to go into complete denial. To just tag along to such a shitty nightclub ... Well, it beggared belief.

When the police arrived - perking up the bouncers' interest even further - it was Glenda who had to talk to them. She had to lead Tony by the arm.

A car had been found. It was crashed in the roadside, in the woods, eighteen miles out of town. Two men had reported it, only a matter of minutes ago. Everything that could be done was being done. Tony listened to the news open-mouthed. The scenario in his head had become private property. Official voices were crackling over the police radio, telling them all that it was true.

Glenda crushed his hand into both of hers as the police car sped them out of town. Really, though, she was appalled at Tony, disgusted with him.

The police in the front were silent, facing forward. They said very little to their passengers. They took their orders and directions from the radio and simply got on with the job. Glenda could appreciate that, though the quiet in the car weighed down on her. But she thought there was something to be gained from doing your job like an automaton and refusing human contact altogether. Simply getting things done. There was something very calming about that.

Now she had cramp all down her left leg. It was as if some-one had taken the muscle and tendons and had tried to plait them up. That's all she needed now. She shifted in her seat and let go of Tony's hands and tried to straighten out the leg, but there wasn't enough room. She looked at the neat, white, shaved nape of the driver's neck and that of the policeman next to him. Memories of some old horror film stirred up in her. They would turn around in their seats to look at their passengers and their faces would drop off, revealing smooth, sinister, egg heads underneath.

The snow was flurrying past the car windows as they left the town behind. Thicker, faster than ever: a gentle onslaught that did nothing to calm her nerves or heart. Tony seemed oblivious.

'I told her to go faster,' he said to Glenda, finding her hand again in the dark. 'I kept her talking on the mobile. I kept phoning her up. That ginger Geoff kept telling me to phone her up again and again and I did. I did what he said. I was phoning her and telling her that she'd be too late. That she would miss your leaving do. She didn't want to miss it. She was yelling and screaming down the phone at me, telling me that she was flooring it. She was going faster and faster and yelling into the phone ...'

Glenda was torn between listening and nodding and hearing it all pour out of him like she knew it ought and telling him to shut up, for now. The police were listening. He'd get himself in bother. Tony was making himself out to be the one to blame. But maybe he was.

He squeezed her hand till she felt the knuckles crack and jar.

'She was hurrying to get to your party, Glenda.'

'All right, Tony.' Shut up now, she thought.

He'd have to save up his words. They would have him talking, giving statements, talking and talking till morning, she knew.

4

Robin watched his wife comfort the barrel-chested man. Then he picked up the book he had been reading when they'd arrived and went through to the kitchen. There he watched the sky start to pinken and lighten over the dark, straggly bushes of the back gardens. He pondered on the oddness of meeting Darren from the department in the twenty-four hour garage and hearing about the accident from him. And then all this. Glenda bringing the person at the epicentre of that disaster back here, to their quiet house.

He pondered it for a while, but then brushed the thoughts away and started up the espresso maker. He let its gurgling steam rinse away the troublesome thoughts.

He'd been drowsing on the chintz settee, like a guard dog, waiting for Glenda to arrive. He'd picked up an old Penguin copy of *The Sandcastle* from a shelf in the study before settling down on the cushions. He hadn't read Murdoch in years and he had forgotten everything about this particular one. It was one of her earlier novels and just the first few pages required - it seemed - immense concentration from him, just to keep up with what was going on and who was who.

Soon he had felt the book slipping out of his fingers, and his body relaxing completely into the sofa and the noises of his dreams lapping over him as the most pressing thing, the most diverting thing ...

Still he kept his vigil up, kept snapping himself awake, forcing his attention back to the Murdoch book, struggling to make sense of it: all her funny characters, her impacted subclauses, her swimming lists of adjectives.

That had been when Glenda turned up, out of the blue, with Tony and the two of them shrouded in disaster.

Another night awake and the bed upstairs untouched.

Once they had managed to pack Tony off to the neat spare room and Glenda was sure that he would be okay left on his own, Robin asked her: 'Why did you never phone me to say all this was going on?'

'I thought about it,' she said. They were in the kitchen and under the harsh yellow lights the skin around her eyes looked pulled tight and greyish. 'I thought about it in the hospital. And I realised I still had my mobile switched on, which is bad. All I could think was that I was probably fucking up someone's dialysis or a life support machine or something ...'

They were both blowing on their espressos and it was almost daylight outside, almost seven. The air was clearing; the garden giving out a chill mist, as if something was exhaling very slowly out there.

It seemed absurd that they were both drinking out of these very small cups, like something out of a dolls' tea party.

'What was it like, out on the road?' Robin asked her.

'God, what do you want? All the details? Do you want to know how much blood there was? How many coppers there were?'

He raised his eyebrows at this outburst.

'I'm sorry,' Glenda said. 'I just don't want to go over it all again.'

She put down her miniature cup and patted his arm and eased past him through the narrow, galley kitchen.

'There's been enough talking about it all night,' she said. 'I'm going up to get a few hours' lie down.'

He nodded.

On her way out of the kitchen she flinched and caught hold of the calf of her left leg. 'Ow. Shit.'

'What is it?' He was rinsing their cups.

'Cramp again. It came on in the police car.'

'Let's see..?' He moved over.

'There's nothing to bloody see,' she said through gritted teeth. 'It's cramp. Ow. Bugger.' She was rubbing at the muscle, stooped over in the doorway and, with a thrill of horror, she realised that she could hardly feel the pressure of her thumb on her leg as it worked.

'Well,' said Robin lazily. 'At least you don't have to go into work tomorrow.'

She looked at him sharply, as if she suspected him of sarcasm.

'I mean it,' he said. 'You'll be dead on your feet tomorrow.'

Glenda shook her head at him, whistling between her teeth. 'You always find just the right thing to say, don't you?'

He winced. 'Let's get up to bed.'

5

Once they were lying side by side in their room, turning off their bedside lamps and realising that it was almost as light with them off, she turned to him and said: 'How come you're reading Iris Murdoch?'

'Hm?' He pretended not to hear.

'You haven't read her in years.'

Facing away from her, Robin smiled to himself. He loved the way that, although she hardly ever read a book herself, Glenda always kept close tabs on his own reading habits.

'I don't know,' he whispered. 'She just came back into my head for some reason.'

Glenda seemed satisfied with that.

He listened to her sigh and roll over.

'I wish I'd stayed in and read a novel,' she said. 'Instead of running about the place in that ridiculous outfit.'

'You looked sensational in that. That's your new outfit. Your I'm-leaving-work-forever-and-I-look-fantastic outfit.'

He could even hear her smile against the pillow, the delicate rustle of the fabric on her face as she grinned. 'Cheers, fella,' she said.

'It's true,' he said. 'You looked great.'

'My leaving do,' she said thoughtfully, after a moment.

They lay awake for a while.

'Did you know Marion well?' he asked at last.

'A bit. She was on the deli counter.'

For some reason that conjured a horrible image in Robin's head. He tried to blot it out, but the next thing he knew he was asleep.

And then it was lunchtime and they had to face the widower all over again.

6

The widower Tony wanted to go straight home. 'Listen, you've been great. I'd still be wandering around, not knowing what was going on, without you, Glenda.' He looked at them through swollen eyes. Robin thought he looked like a skinned rabbit.

'I've got to go home, though,' Tony said. 'The police are coming round again this afternoon. There's stuff to sort out ...'

Glenda asked if he wanted her to come with him.

Robin watched Tony open his mouth, deciding.

Of course he wanted her to.

Left alone downstairs in Tony's house (she was about to call it Marion's house, but she went back and erased that before she could stop herself) Glenda suddenly felt like phoning her husband.

As Tony went hunting through papers and address books upstairs, Glenda wanted to get on the phone and ask Robin: If I'd had a child ... If in some hypothetical world ... I'd had a grown-up child from a first marriage and you didn't get on with them – and then, if I'd died suddenly – would you wait almost a day before trying to contact them? Would you get flustered and cross because you couldn't find their address anywhere?

It was the kind of hypothetical that Glenda often put to her husband, and she would make them so detailed and involved that he would lose track (mind elsewhere already) and she would have to start again.

She hadn't known Marion had had an earlier husband. Tony had told her that Marion had divorced him years ago, in her twenties, and she had a daughter she never really saw. It astonished Glenda that there could be so little contact, and the chance that Tony might not even have some note of the daughter's current address. Glenda was amazed that it had taken so long – a couple of tense hours back in Tony and Marion's house – for Tony to even remember the daughter.

As she so often did, Glenda decided it was something she couldn't ever understand. She herself didn't have kids. Maybe it was one of those things people who'd had kids would know about; how their kids could slip away, under the radar. Maybe it was normal. She didn't think so, though.

Upstairs Tony was crashing about. She heard a few muffled swear words, cupboard doors banging, desk drawers, and heaps of paper being flung down.

Glenda had been left alone, presumably, until she was need-ed again for consolation purposes, or to do something imme-diate and practical. She had already talked with the coroner and the undertaker. Those services had been incredibly swift. She was secretly appalled at how easily and simply it could all be arranged. Everyone was so professional, with their patter down perfect. Even the police, calling back again, hadn't had that much to say. They said it and they went, leaving the distracted Tony to get on with the rest. 'We're sure you've got a lot to sort out,' was how the police-woman had put it, showing herself out of the front door.

It was when they had left that Tony had remembered Clare, Marion's daughter. To give him credit, he had looked shocked at himself, that he'd taken so long to think of her. She lived in Glasgow, with a boyfriend that no one had met.

Glenda felt helpless and useless on their settee, waiting for him. She wondered if she should tidy round. The house had been left Friday-morning-messy: the accumulated junk of a week for two working people left strewn through every room. She thought about tactfully slipping the women's magazines off the coffee table into a rack or onto a shelf. She noticed a knitting bag stowed by the side of the settee and wondered where she would hide that.

Then she decided to do nothing. Such a project could get out of hand and Glenda would find herself applying her grimly efficient organisational skills in trying to erase every sign of Marion as a living presence in the house.

That would do no good. There was just so much of her. Marion was on photos on the living room wall unit. In flowery frames there were snaps of Marion and Tony at different do's, weddings and Christmases, on beaches, hugging each other, smiling and mugging down through the years.

Glenda had never really thought of Marion doing these kind of things, in photographs that looked so different to Glenda's own. This is what ordinary, happily married life looks like, she thought. You have a nice time somewhere, take photos, pick out the best ones and frame them on your wall.

Glenda thought about her own front room. On their walls they had three Paul Klees in silver frames and a dark and smudgy print of a wistful Virginia Woolf, because Robin claimed she looked like his mother in that shot. Robin had no surviving pictures of his mother.

At least the numbness down her leg had cleared up. That must have been a twinge of stress. Or maybe just the cold. Anyway, it had resolved into a smattering of pins and needles, which stretched round to the bottom of her back now. Tony and Marion's settee was much too soft and squashy – one of those where once you'd sat down you'd have to struggle to get up again.

Funny she'd never been round here before. The only time she saw her work mates was in public. In the shop and those irregular nights out that she generally dreaded.

As supervisor I probably held myself aloof, Glenda thought.

Even subconsciously. Not getting too involved in their lives, in order to protect myself. I drew some reasonable lines. I was keeping my work mates and my real friends quite separate.

But then she thought: Who are my real friends? And she realised that she hadn't had any in years. It was a bleak, nasty little thought.

Just then Tony came crashing down the stairs with a tattered address book, diary and a heap of frayed papers. He looked at her apologetically. He also looked handsome, for a second, and she caught a glimpse of what Marion must have seen in him. He had changed into dark jeans and a black jumper (for mourning and grieving? she wondered. Had it been on purpose?) He was sitting now and roving through his mass of papers, exactly like a man used to collating paperwork and extracting just the right information.

Glenda remembered asking him, absurdly, chattily, in the hospital, what his profession was and he'd explained, in equally absurd detail, as they waited on plastic chairs, that his work involved organising the shipping of new cars from Holland. Now Glenda had heard all about how Tony's company kept fobbing him off with Manuals instead of Automatics, slipping a few extra in each freight of cars on the ferry. And his customers wanted Automatics and his first loyalty was to his good, loyal, steady stream of customers, some of them collectors. Tony's ire at his company's underhandedness struck Glenda as oddly sharp, given the context.

He looked up at her and said, 'I phoned Clare. I found her number in last year's desk diary.'

'You've phoned her?'

He nodded. 'I wasn't on for long. She didn't really want to talk to me, did she?'

'How did she take it?'

Tony shook his head. 'God knows. There'd been a lot of ructions between them. They parted on bad terms, the last time Marion went up there, to Glasgow, to try to talk to her. Marion thought Clare hated her.'

Glenda frowned. For God's sake, don't tell her that, she thought. Just tell Clare that her mother loved her and everything was okay at the end. At times like this, no one wanted to hear the complicated, real life stuff. They didn't want reminding that things get left unsettled and now never will be settled. They want everything clear and precise. They go back to wanting to think the world works as it did when they were kids: that love is clear-cut, unconditional and that it's everlasting. She almost wanted to instruct Tony on how he should talk to his stepdaughter and what he should be allowed to say.

'She's going to travel down,' he said. 'Tomorrow, she reckons. It's about ten hours on the train. Worse, with the speed restrictions.'

Glenda flinched at that last phrase. Tony didn't even realise what he'd said. Yet she thought of him in the middle of last night, telling her how he'd urged Marion to drive faster and faster and how it was all down to him.

Glenda had never seen anyone look and behave so helplessly as he had last night. She couldn't remember holding

118

anyone so hard and close, especially in public. Without even thinking she had broken out of her natural reserve. She had cast aside what Robin mockingly called her natural ironic distance.

'What's an ironic distance?' she would ask her husband.

'Why, it's no distance at all,' he'd say.

She had rocked Tony like a baby. Seeing him now, a stranger again in a black jumper, fiddling with private papers, she realised she was blushing. Her fingers had stroked his neck, had squeezed his sides, squashing his flesh to the bone.

'I'm glad Clare's coming down,' he said. 'I don't know if she'll stay here. She never thought much of me.'

'Well ...' said Glenda. 'People behave differently at these kind of things. Better than themselves, if you see what I mean.'

He nodded blankly. 'Will you come to the funeral? The cremation, I mean. You and ...'

'Robin,' she supplied. 'Yes, of course.'

It was to be on Friday. Not too far off. Clean as a whistle. No fuss. Something dignified and not too fancy. Tony had spoken curtly down the phone to the undertaker, hardly seeming to consider the specifics.

'There's no will,' Tony said. 'I know for a fact she never made one. Oh, she said daft things like she wanted "When I Am An Angel" by Things Fall Apart playing at her service, but nothing really practical ...'

Glenda, of course, had made a will. She didn't know what to say. 'I'm sure it will all be fairly straightforward.'

'That's all I want it to be,' he said.

She felt uncomfortable then. He'd stopped thanking her and apologising. He'd also stopped crying, several hours ago.

He said, 'I remember Clare staying with us once. She must have been nineteen or so. At college. And she asked Marion straight out, over dinner, did she want burying or cremating? She was a morbid little thing, that Clare. And Marion was quite hurt by the question. As if she thought Clare was saying that she wanted her mother dead. Well, Marion could snap back ... She could have a quick tongue on her. And she shouted: "Clare – you can bloody well eat me for all I care, you callous little madam." And off stomped Marion, and Clare bursts into tears.'

Now Tony was smiling off into the distance. 'I didn't know where to put myself.'

Here's when the person starts turning into a whole load of anecdotes, Glenda thought. Tony will be trying to remember as many things like that as he can. Just to keep the sound of her voice in his head.

But there was something a little bit cold about the recollection, too. As if Tony was too ready to consign these moments to history. But I'm being harsh, Glenda thought. I don't know how I'd react if I lost Robin. I really don't. What if I couldn't think up any anecdotes? What if there was nothing at all I could latch onto and bring out? She had a moment of panic about this.

There would be a hell of a lot of ironic distance to cover.

Could I bring myself, really, to think of fond, sweet little anecdotes to remember Robin by?

Tony had his back to her, rooting through a shelfful of old vinyl LPs in the wall unit. He told her he was looking for the Greatest Hits of Things Fall Apart. He was sure they must still have it somewhere.

Vaguely Glenda could recall the song.

8

Glenda had come home wanting to flop straight into bed.

'I should sue you for neglect,' Robin told her.

'Have you just been sat around all day doing nothing?' she asked. 'You could have got some groceries in.'

'Working,' he said. 'It doesn't look very spectacular from the outside, but there's all sorts going on in here.' He tapped his thinning pate.

'Great,' she said and let him rub the back of her neck. 'Robin, how come we don't have pictures of ourselves on the walls? Tony and Marion do. All over their house.'

'Ah,' he said. 'That's because we already know what we look like. I'd recognise you in a million years.'

'Hm.' She wasn't willing to be amused. 'But we change,

don't we? It would be nice to have them up. To remember different things. To show people.'

'I don't think we've changed so much.'

She had hold of his hands, kneading them as he grasped her. 'Marion had a daughter, it turns out,' she told him. 'Grown up. In Glasgow. There'd been fights.'

'Oh yes?'

'Tony had to talk to her and she hates his guts, apparently.'

'I take it he's not her father.'

'Step.'

'Hm. Well, he'll have a few things like that to face before the week's out. Someone dies and leaves a hole. All the past comes rushing in to fill it up. Tony's standing right in the way of that.'

Glenda was listening, imagining Tony standing in a roomful of mucky flood water. Standing on his too-soft settee. The water bringing in all this tidal filth and slurry.

'You could be sucked down forever, left like that,' Robin said. 'It's good you've been there to help him. How's your leg?'

'The cramps have gone. Bit stiff still.'

'Hm.'

He packed her off to bed. He took her a Lemsip and his

heart went out to her, sitting up in their bed, with the top end of the duvet folded back just so. She looked like a little girl, a single clip keeping her hair back, the straps of her nightie so neat.

'Will madam be requiring anything else?'

She shook her head and smiled.

'Madam doesn't require a little cuddle?'

'No thanks.'

Actually, she wouldn't have minded just that. But Glenda knew that what Robin meant by a cuddle wasn't her idea of one. It would turn into sex, no matter how worn out they were. In a way, she should be glad they still had a sex life like that, after all the years between them. But sometimes she just wanted a hug, just the ordinary contact.

Really, she blamed Robin for always turning it into sex. And naturally, he blamed her. 'I get a hard-on just looking! I always do! I always will! I love you! That's what happens!'

He was so simple. It was so straightforward to him. She knew she ought to be grateful.

'Okay,' he said, backing away. She knew he'd be retreating to his study. 'No cuddle tonight, then.'

She wriggled back down in their bed as he clicked off the light.

'No cuddle tonight,' she agreed and was worried that it was such a relief.

Kim

1

Through the middle of the store the glass elevator went up and down, all day long. It was one of the new things they had put in when the department store was refitted.

Quite a show-piece.

It would rise up through the levels, from the ground floor foodhall and Menswear, soaring up to Ladies and then right up to soft furnishings, household goods.

It connected Geoff in Menswear with Kim upstairs and he would use it, when he could, to go and visit her. This was something he took every opportunity to do.

Vistas of immaculate consumables would open out to the occupants of the new glass lift. To the onlooker on steady ground, all the mechanisms and cogs that made the elevator work were miraculously visible, under the platform on which the occupants stood.

When it was first in use, people gathered to stare at the see-through lift. Eventually they got used to it. It was just like any normal lift. But on Tuesday morning it became novel again. Tuesday morning was when it broke down for the very first time, and with three schoolboys on board. Three school truants were wedged solid halfway between Menswear and Ladies' shoes and everyone could see them, looking bewildered. One of them seemed tearful.

Geoff from Menswear was busily folding an Extra Extra Large shirt carefully and patting it into a large carrier for a lady and he was working alongside the young, well-spoken Peter when he became aware of the kerfuffle over by the lift area.

A gaggle of shoppers had gathered there, cooing and interested.

Straight away, and with sales staff intuition, Geoff knew that something was up. Shoppers wouldn't gather like that unless someone had collapsed or otherwise disgraced themselves in public.

How easily shoppers forgot their cares, he thought, and everything that they were here to do, at the very first hint of disaster or outrage. They must come out looking for it, he thought.

A woman hurried up with a four pack of black cotton socks.

'There's someone stuck in there,' she confided. 'One of them's having a panic attack. It's three boys. By all rights, they should be in school.'

'Stuck in the lift?' Geoff asked, with a shudder.

'And you can see them in there,' the woman said. 'It's horrible to see. You can't hear them, but you can see them, like fish in a tank. Really, it's cruel, but everyone's looking.'

Geoff's assistant Peter was suddenly keen to leave his till unmanned.

'Let Security sort it,' Geoff told him.

'They might need help,' Peter said stiffly. It was true, Security in the store wasn't all that good.

'I'll go,' said Geoff, leaving the murmuring Menswear queue to Peter, who scowled.

Geoff had to fight through the crowd at the other side of men's underwear and socks. When he looked up he could see the bottom of the lift and three pairs of legs, going nowhere.

Expert on the store's layout (and feeling just like an action hero in a big film) he took the escalator at a run. Much safer than a lift anyway, he thought, statistically speaking.

He hurried up to Ladieswear, where a similar crowd had bunched itself by Lingerie. This gathering was even more excited, because they had the three boys' faces at knee level and it was quite true: while two of the faces were mystified and cross, the third one, the youngest-looking, was tearful.

He was beating his palms on the glass. Geoff watched his wild red face and the white of the flat of his hands as he bashed away on the glass.

He'll be smashing that, Geoff thought. And then we'll know about it.

In Ladieswear, Kim was already taking charge, leading across two of the security men in their tight beige trousers and their ill-fitting hats. Her arms were folded as they cleared a space amongst the customers to examine the lift's workings.

126

Kim's face was pinched up with irritation and concern.

Geoff touched her elbow.

How competent she looked, her hair all pulled up with that clip, her jacket and skirt pressed just so. Geoff thought that everyone must be relieved at the sight of her, striding up like this.

'They'll have been pushing all the buttons at once,' she sighed. 'That's what the kids always do. They think it's a toy. I've stood and watched them. They've been up and down in that all morning. It serves them right, really.'

'That one's got himself upset,' Geoff said. 'He'll have a hard time living this down with his pals.'

Kim tutted.

The security men were fiddling with a panel of controls set into the glass doors. Kim hoped they knew what they were doing, and not just pressing any old thing.

'Look,' said Geoff. 'He's getting hysterical in there, now.'

All the onlookers craned to see the boy. His two trapped friends were laughing at him. The glass muffled noises within the lift, but it was clear he was being taunted.

'They'll have his life,' Geoff said.

'It's not fair,' said Kim. 'Anyone can get claustrophobic.'

The ladies around them were sighing at the boy's face. 'Isn't it a shame?' someone said. 'He's a lovely looking lad, as well.'

At last, after a good deal of pressing things, one of the security guards did something right. The new glass lift shuddered and then, by shaky degrees, started to rise.

Gradually it settled into its proper space, flush with Lingerie.

'Ah, look,' said Kim. 'He's wet himself.'

Everyone was looking. The security men were prying open the doors. As they did and a gap started to open up, the raucous laughter of two of the boys came braying out. Also, the wails and sobs of the one who'd panicked.

'My job now,' said Kim determinedly. 'They've arrived in my department.'

Usually, Robin thought, as he watched Kim stride grimly forth, it would be the manageress's job. Kim had effectively promoted herself.

The three boys tumbled out of the escalator. The two unharmed ones shouted and laughed, and then they took one look at the security men and small crowd. They turned and fled.

One of the beige-uniformed men yelled, 'Hoy!' half-heartedly and set off in chase.

Kim was left to prop up the crying boy, who was older than he looked and having some trouble standing straight.

'I'm going to be sick,' he told her. A larger space opened up in the crowd.

'There's nothing to see here now,' Geoff called out, thinking he should do something.

'I'm really going to be sick,' the boy said again.

Kim took a tight hold of him, by elbow and wrist and she started to march him away across Lingerie.

'It's all right,' she told the boy savagely, wanting to shake him. 'You're out of there now.'

An elderly lady was standing with Geoff. She was one of the last to drift away. 'Bless him,' she said. 'Fancy messing yourself in front of everyone in a big shop like this.'

Geoff nodded. 'It's not something you see every day.'

******

In the staff room Kim took the boy's name, address and home phone number.

He was shivering and guilty-looking, exactly as if he'd been caught stealing goods.

While Kim went to phone his mother, she left him to take off his soggy combat pants. She gave him a handful of rough paper towels to swab himself down with.

At the door she bumped into Geoff. 'Can you fetch him a pair of trousers from Menswear?'

'What size?' he said. 'What kind?'

She looked impatient. 'Oh, anything. He should be glad of anything. I'm going to phone his mother.'

'Right.' Geoff looked across at the boy. 'About thirty waist, I'd have thought.'

'It's not a fitting, Geoff,' Kim hissed. 'Just get him something to cover himself up with.'

'Right.'

'And we'll bill his mother when she comes to pick him up.' She turned on the boy, who looked bewildered in his tee shirt and boxer shorts, a handful of paper towels and long, pale legs. 'Just you sit there and get yourself together,' she snapped.

Geoff hurried off to fetch a pair of trousers. When he got there blond Peter raised an eyebrow. 'Poor kid's wet himself,' Geoff explained, picking out some jeans. He didn't even know what a kid of that age would like to wear. Probably Geoff would be taking him something old-mannish and wrong.

'Wet himself?'

'Kim's looking after him,' Geoff said.

Peter said, 'No wonder.'

Geoff gave him a funny look and hurried back to Ladieswear. Bit of excitement in here this morning, he was thinking. Well, it's not every day. That lift'll be out of action for a while.

******

Then they had to sit and wait for the mother turning up. It was their break anyway, and Geoff and Kim ended up sitting with the snivelling boy. He was across the room from them in brand new, too large jeans, hanging his head.

'I really admire how cool you are in emergencies,' Geoff told her, softly enough so the boy wouldn't hear.

'Well ...' she said. She'd perked up slightly and didn't seem so harried. 'It wasn't really an emergency. No one was really hurt.'

'They could have been.' Geoff nodded at the pale boy. 'He could have psychic damage. That's a terrible thing. He's most probably marked for life.'

Kim looked at the boy with new interrest.

'I think you were great with him. The way you talked to him and calmed him down,' said Geoff. 'It really worked. You were a real professional. I'm not sure I'd have coped as well as you. You know, I reckon you could become a professional counsellor or something.'

'You do?'

'You can do evening classes or something in that, can't you?' Geoff mused. 'You should look into them, I think, Kim. I think you've got something. I think you've got the gift of empathy.'

Kim shrugged. 'Oh ... I don't know about that.'

131

'That lad's right as rain now, after just about dying of shock, and that's all down to you and your quick thinking. I didn't do anything.'

'All I did was get him into a new pair of trousers and phoned his mum,' she said.

'I still think you were great,' Geoff said.

'Well, thank you, Geoff.'

'I think you're a wonderful woman. A very special person.'

Kim turned to look at him; a sceptical look, as if he was having her on.

'I mean it,' he said. 'A special lady.'

'Well.' She smiled tightly. 'I do my best.'

'And I love you, Kim. I've fallen in love with you.'

'You what?'

Across the room, the boy flinched. He was listening in.

'I talked with your mother last night in Sainsburys. I've felt like this since I've known you. Your mum said it would be all right to ... to declare my feelings like this.'

'In the staff common room?'

He nodded.

'With some stupid kid listening in?'

The kid looked away.

'My mother put you up to this? My mother did?'

Kim's voice was cracking out like a whip.

'Honestly, Geoff,' she said.

He shushed her.

'Don't you shush me.'

The door opened and in came one of the security men, looking pleased with himself, leading in a woman in an anorak. 'Daniel?' she shrilled. 'What have you been up to now?'

'Mam, I ...'

'You dirty little devil. Wetting yourself.'

'Mam ...'

She scooted over to the boy on noisy slingbacks. She rounded on the shocked-looking Geoff and Kim.

'Those aren't his jeans. Did you give him those?'

'Yes,' said Kim in a determined voice. 'His wet ones are in that carrier.'

'Marvellous. And you'll be expecting me to pay for them, will you?'

'Well, yes.'

'And I can't afford them! I wasn't expecting to pay for new jeans for this little devil. And now I'll have to, I suppose. I can't afford to buy clothes in a shop like this. How would you like it, eh? How would you like to have something foisted on you like that? Something you never even asked for?'

Then she was hugging her son and she was crying as well.

2

The dogs had run wild through the house.

There were nine of them, all different types, sizes and temperaments (from toylike up to horse-sized, from sweet as a puppy to downright nasty.) Sometimes Kim would swear down there was more of them: hundreds of the things in her house, demanding attention, jumping up, chewing furniture and rugs, shitting everywhere.

Tonight her mother had let things slip (again). She had left the doors open and the things had run wild.

A line from that stupid song kept going through her head, about 'Who let the dogs out?' And there was no use wondering, because she knew it was her mother. Elsa had been unfocused and neglectful just lately. In fact, she'd been so erratic she was horrible to live with.

Kim could just about deal with the animals when they were well behaved and coralled. But not like this. Not when they overran each neat room, squeezing her out of her own home. The house was starting to take on a shabby look, like the home of two old spinsters and Kim didn't care to look too hard.

She would leave it all for her mother to sort out, whenever she chose to come back from her hospital visiting.

All Kim had done was laboriously unpack the groceries in the kitchen. All the tins in the right cupboard, everything in the correct order in the fridge. That was something else. Her mother had left without a word, without even offering to help unpack.

Elsa was hopeless at that anyway, too hasty and disorganised. She put half-used tubs of margarine and lemon halves to the back of the fridge, behind the new things. That way disaster lay, Kim knew.

The weird thing had been how her mother had walked through the house while the dogs were going wild and having free rein, and she'd never even commented on it. She had come in and then left again, like a ghost. Like a woman with a mission.

Well, Kim could have a mission, too. It wasn't like she couldn't find things to entertain her. Actually, she was glad of the quiet.

She went upstairs.

She took off her pinching shoes and rubbed her toes in her tights as she waited for the computer to load and connect itself. Her toes were slightly damp. She cricked them in her palm as the modem chirruped and bonged.

She liked the noise it made as it dialled itself up. It was a busy, thoughtful noise. It sounded, with its considered pauses and gaps, exactly like somebody trying to remember something.

3

It was Saturday morning.

In Ladieswear Kim found herself dealing with more refunds than she had time or energy for. It was as bad as Boxing Day, with this queue of women and their crumpled, used plastic bags and their dissatisfied looks and their hunting out of days-old receipts.

Refunds was always a chore. Sometimes Kim enjoyed the power of it. She would take the unsatisfactory garment and examine it, just to make sure the customer was bringing it back in exactly the condition in which she'd bought it.

Oh, there had been some lovely, scandalous scenes like that. The woman she'd caught with last year's summer dress, who was claiming, bare-faced, that she'd bought it just last week, and she wanted the full value back because it was tight under the armpits. That time, Kim was armed with all the facts and had the delicious task of telling the woman – the felon! – that this was from last summer's stock and therefore she, the criminal, must have been wearing this dress for a full year before returning it so blithely. Oh, the woman had been mortified and she'd taken the garment away again without a word. She'd skulked away from Refunds and everyone had looked.

Kim knew all the tricks they used. Sponging out the armpits of worn outfits after wearing them for some night out, bringing them back the next day, as if this was some sort of dress hire shop.

They'd stop at nothing, some of these customers.

Before beginning here, six years ago, Kim had thought the clientele at this store – this grand, glassy edifice, all clean green and white, all spartan, pastel colours – would be a little cut above.

What she'd learned was that people were the same all over. This had been disappointing. If you were the one behind the counter, there would always be a queue of punters trying to get one over on you.

But Kim was sharp. She knew the ins and outs and all the scams. She could see them coming a mile off.

Not today, though. Today she was thick-headed and her blood felt thin in her veins. When she stood still she swayed on her court shoes and she had to grip the counter top for minutes at a time, resting her parched eyes when she could.

She shouldn't have been out so late. She'd barely slept.

But, she told herself, she hadn't had much choice. It had been an evening out with colleagues from work, and she would rather die than miss even a moment of that. It was a part of the job, that's how she saw it.

You had to be there on nights like that because that's when you got to mix with colleagues and superiors. That's when people let down their guards and when they would notice you as a real human being.

Mixing in company like that was the surefire way of moving up the company ladder.

Kim had worked hard to make sure that she had become a good mixer.

Besides, she couldn't have left any earlier last night. She wouldn't have gone back home in a cab by herself. Some of those drivers were like maniacs.

She'd had an arrangement with ginger Geoff about the two of them sharing a taxi. He lived near enough to her to make splitting the fare worth his while.

He thought he might be getting something else, too.

Ginger Geoff thought that, every time Kim needed him to squire her around the town like that, he was getting one step closer to seeing her staff discount underwear.

Well, the thought of that could give her the screaming abdabs if she dwelled on it.

Still, she knew how to handle the likes of Geoff and his obsession with her. She knew how to keep him on a short leash.

Why can't people just be nice friends? she wondered.

Why can't people just be nice?

Even her mother, who lived with her and who ought to be past all of that, got a twinkle in her eye when she talked about old Mr Pastry in the Sheltered accomodation.

Kim's mother was round that old folks' home more often than need be, doing her voluntary visiting with her animals (the pets cheered the old people up, apparently.) She was there with her dogs more than her rota strictly required. And Kim knew that it was because of the flirting that went on between her mother and the eighty-year-old man her mother called Mr Pastry. She called him that because he had very cold hands, by all reports.

Kim thought it was all a bit lubricious and didn't like to talk about it. Her mother was over there this morning, with a Border Collie and a Shitzu, undoubtedly making smutty small talk with this tireless old devil.

Kim changed the till roll, spooling out yards of voided slips, all joined up in a perfect, tidy ribbon. It would soon be her break. Earlier she had set aside a bottle of apple-flavoured sparkling water and a luxury prawn mayonnaise sandwich. Now she wished she hadn't elected for prawns.

She had to pass through Menswear to get to the staffroom.

Geoff was there in a Homer Simpson tie, putting hooded tops back in order from Small up to Extra Large. What on earth were they doing selling hooded tops?

'Isn't it funny without Glenda here?' he asked as she went by.

'Oh? I hadn't really noticed.'

'Or Marion,' he said. 'She's not turned up, apparently.'

Marion was on the deli counter usually. That had been a covetable post when it was first brought in. But Kim thought that Marion smelled of cooked meats and cheeses and she didn't think that was very nice, carrying that away with you.

Kim wasn't in the mood to talk to Geoff. She imagined she was dehydrating on the spot and thought longingly of her apple-flavoured water.

She looked at him narrowly. Last night he had disappointed her, asking her into his shabby, stuccoed house with the messy hedge outside. Offering her instant coffee with bourbons. She had turned him down flat. She'd seen the style of his kitchen once and wouldn't have been able to face it at three in the morning. Rings of scum on mugs that were meant to be clean. A Britney Spears calendar in the hallway. No proper pictures of scenery, or anything.

'Fancy Glenda not saying a proper goodbye to anyone,' she said. 'And she left her coat behind with all her presents and cards. Shows how much she valued them. They were still in the cloakroom, unclaimed. She must have been desperate to get away last night.'

Geoff shrugged and there was mischief in his eyes. 'With Tony,' he said.

'Now, Geoff,' Kim said. 'That's how low idle gossip begins.'

He looked shame-faced for a moment. 'It's true though, isn't it? And I always thought that Glenda had a look about her ...'

'A look?'

'Like she might, you know ...'

'What, Geoff?'

'That she might be a bit easy or something.'

Kim felt her nostrils flare. She didn't think that much of Glenda – especially after her nasty outburst last night – but she wasn't about to listen to mucky talk from Geoff.

'Is that how you think about women, then?' she asked, in a scandalized tone. 'Do you rank them like that? Easy, all the way up to completely impregnable?'

He looked dismayed. 'Of course not.'

She glanced at her watch and realised she had wasted precious time on him. She would ditch the prawns. Get a refund. Have a banana for the potassium. She started clipping away, saying to him, without looking back: 'For that, you can take me to lunch today. I finish at One.'

'So do I!' he called out, tangling up the hangers on the hooded tops in his eagerness. 'I'll take you somewhere swanky. To make up for...'

But she was gone.

'... everything,' he said.

Kim, he thought happily, was the type of woman who needed things making up to her. She didn't really know it herself. She wore a lifetime of disappointments as tidily as she wore her staff uniform; her blazer and patterned cotton skirt. Geoff knew this about her and still thought he could do something about it. He hated the thought of Kim rattling about in that old house of hers with her tiny old mother and all those animals.

Kim's mother had yards of mackerel-coloured hair heaped up on her withered head and stuck with pins the length of knitting needles. He'd never been inside their house, but once, in an unguarded moment, Kim had said it was like a zoo. And her, sensitive and allergic to everything! She needed rescuing from all of that, he knew. She wouldn't want people thinking she was a funny spinster, stuck in with her mother. But why couldn't she loosen up a little? It was because she was a career woman and proud of it. She was a proper lady.

Geoff went back to his tills, where the blond boy Peter was standing idly by, staring into space. 'Time was,' Geoff told him, 'they'd have been packed five deep at this counter on a Saturday morning. Oh, this is shocking, lad. You've no idea how much we've gone into decline.'

Peter had a discreet gold earring and a blond goatee beard. 'Hm?' he went.

'I said, you wouldn't have had time to stand around posing, not back in the heyday.'

'Have you heard?' Peter asked. He had a posh accent, Peter. He really charmed the wives who came in buying socks. 'Store card, madam?' All that.

Sent them away smiling. Got away with murder as a result.

'It's going through the shop like wildfire,' Peter was saying.

Geoff chuckled. 'What is? Foot and mouth? That's all we need. We'll have to dig a deep pit out back and shove in anyone who drools.'

Peter was serious. 'Glenda phoned up and it's gone right round the shop. The news.'

'What news, lad?'

'Marion off baked meats and cheeses. She was killed last night. Killed outright in a car crash.'

'She couldn't have been,' Geoff started.

'She was! Glenda saw her body ... She went to identify her ...'

Geoff was trying to piece it together, knowing it made sense before he even got the story all lined up. He swore. And – hating himself for thinking it, but thinking it never-theless – he realised that Marion's death was all Kim would want to talk about, all through lunch time. No matter how much he tried to divert her, that's all that would be on the menu today.

4

'What you need, Mum, is music all day long. I'm telling you. That's what you want.

'Look. I'll show you how to tune in the radio. Here's Radio One. It's music all day on that. You'll like that. It's be non-stop company all day and that's what you need.

'That's what you need more than anything now, Mum.

'I only wish I could be here all day with you. But they've given me all the compassionate leave they can and they've been very good about it. Better than most stores would have been.

'But look ... Radio One will be good company for you...'

Did I really think that would be true? Kim wondered.

I was not quite thirty, I was stupid.

I was thinking that Mum would really want to listen to pop music all day long and that that would have taken her out of herself and reassured her.

A woman of sixty listening to Radio One while she was grieving, for god's sake! What was I thinking of?

Kim was in the Slug and Lettuce at lunch time. Ginger Geoff had gone upstairs to the loo, leaving Kim with her salad, suddenly thinking about the days after her father's death, some seven years ago. Kim had strived to get her mother to manage.

This was all Geoff's fault, this. Rabbiting on about dead Marion.

This was why Kim was thinking about how people cope.

Back then Kim had had to leave her mum alone all day in the house. But Kim hadn't had any choice. Life was going to change out of all recognition for her mother. Someone had punched it out of all shape and it was up to her mother to deal with that alone. The two of them in that big house had new spaces to fill without Dad there.

And we've managed, Kim thought, through the years since.

Kim sat on the grey settee by the fake log fire and stirred her cappuccino, wondering at herself of seven years ago and how she could have thought listening to Radio One might help her mum.

Now she thought, I have no idea what Mum did do with those hours while I was at work in the store. In the time she had before she started in with all her animals, devoting her care and attention to the world's mutts and strays.

But I was thirty and selfish, with a career to get on with.

For as long as she could remember, Kim had been looking back on younger versions of herself, becoming embarrassed by them. Yet she was always determined, too, not to look back at them for too long. She wanted to push on, instead, to find new mistakes to make. New things to put her foot into. She serially disowned those clumsy, earlier selves.

Back then, she couldn't have done anything for her mum because she hadn't understood the grieving process she was going through. Couldn't fathom it. Thirty odd years with the same man. Kim didn't like to think what that meant, even now. The piling up of stuff it would make and what it would feel like, all tumbling down.

She watched the lunchtime crowd at the blond wood and marble bar, and the waiter going about with food on large plates, nimbly setting them down and returning to the bar. Everything like clockwork in here. The air busy with chatter and the warbling of mobile phones. The steady drone of low-key dance music.

You've got to stop these morbid thoughts, she told herself. If you actually say anything about what you're thinking, Geoff is going to think you're peculiar.

Not that you're out to impress him exactly and certainly not to hook him ... But you don't want him to start thinking you're strange. You don't want him to stop paying his attentions to you (Now this thought surprised her.)

So you mustn't let slip that the news of Marion's sudden, brutal, off-the-wall death has set you tripping your own morbid way down memory lane to Dad's ending up how he did.

It didn't fit with the kind of person she was meant to be. The person in the lintless uniform at the clutter-free counter. The woman who ate only pre-prepared meals from the foodhall because she disliked the mess and palaver of cooking.

Kim didn't want anyone knowing that she slept at night and dreamed of death and disease and terrible things and these thoughts were never far from her.

When she sold her pristine garments, folding them perfect into branded carrier bags, and then when she looked up into the faces of her customers, handing their packages over, she wasn't usually thinking: Oh, you'll look smart in that. Or: That must be a lovely new outfit you'll enjoy wearing at a wedding or on a holiday. Instead Kim was imagining the customer bleeding through the clean fabric and staining it indelibly. She was thinking of them being found somewhere, chopped up, smashed and spattered and wearing the new garment for the first time in a ditch.

146

She could hardly look at new clothes without thinking of the flesh underneath. How it would rupture, burst and stain the cloth. How easy that was. And how inevitable.

Now Geoff was up in the lavs, stumbling through the four or five heavy doors on the way, and up the pine stairs. Kim could have a breather and calmly sip her frothy coffee and swab her lips with a napkin to take off the trace of chocolate powder. Coolly she could look down the menu again, to pass the time; its familiar list of meaty wings, beef nachos and filo parcels.

She was calming herself, ready for Geoff coming back. He would be eager to talk even more about Marion and her untimely demise. He'd be all moist-eyed. He'd be saying how it was only this Monday gone that he'd been at her counter and she'd been chatting away to him as she sliced a huge block of orange cheese.

How she was always such a card and how he'd been telling her husband Tony last night, to urge her on through his mobile to hurry up and get there. How it could even be partly Geoff's fault that she was dead.

That's what Geoff said he kept coming back to: that terrible thought that had struck him, just after Peter at the Menswear counter had told him.

And he'd dwelled on it while he was waiting for Kim to come off on her lunch hour. He'd had the horrible, lurching, sickening thought that Marion had been killed because everyone in the noodle bar had been shouting down the phone at her. Telling her to push herself faster and faster on the icy country roads.

Before Geoff came back down to sit on the grey settee opposite her and before he started going on again in this vein – his voice breaking, his eyes becoming redder – Kim wanted to push her own awful thoughts back. Just so she wouldn't blurt them out at him. Just so she wouldn't suddenly go into one and scream and jeer at him: What? You think this is bad on you? Having to think about this shit now because Marion's dead? I think about death and all sorts all the time, you complacent ginger shit.

The thoughts you're having now – and yes, all the guilt and the sickness – I have that ten times as bad every waking hour, Geoff. That's how I live.

And Kim wasn't coming out with that at any cost. She drank her coffee, cool enough now, and waited for him, and soon she was on a more even keel.

5

Upstairs Geoff was having a sit down in a cubicle.

Hey, there wasn't a scrap of graffiti in here. None of that disgusting mess you often saw in the men's stalls, different places. None of that filth.

He'd once seen one thing, downstairs in the basement of a family pizza place and it was like, the worst thing he'd ever seen. It had said something like, 'I make my three-year-old daughter lick my stiff cock.' That was it. Just like it was someone showing off.

Other of these people scrawled advertisements for themselves, bragging about their endowments and sometimes there was a time and place suggested as an afterthought. Not on that one in the pizza parlour, though. Just a single, bragging statement that Geoff had read as he sat on the bog and it had made him sick to the stomach.

Places for men's secrets, these. The likes of things that ladies like Kim downstairs in the cafe bar need never have to know about or see. And it was men like him, like Geoff, who were made to shield her from knowing about stuff like that going on. It was all he was made for.

When he saw Kim it was like she was crying out for that kind of protection. Never mind what she actually said or how she tried to cover her hurt and her distress all up. He could read her deeper than that and she was really saying that the world was too horrible and cruel and that everyone was so selfish and that she needed someone, really, to stop her knowing that. To wedge their way between her and the world. If only she knew it.

He fiddled with the bog roll. Discarded the first couple of sheets that someone else might have touched. Used the ones after that.

Geoff wasn't a clever man. He knew that. He didn't have to be. Something in him, some gut-level-Geoff knew in all his body what Kim wanted and needed and it was this Geoff that he listened to. He knew he was talking about Marion's death too much. They had only been sitting down for half an hour on their settees, across the coffee table from each other, and he had bored and upset himself, let alone Kim. He had been roving over the little news they had about last night.

149

All they had, really, were scraps. The bare minimum of detail about the tragedy, passed down by word of mouth.

Wisha wisha wisha went the bog paper against his arse.

They didn't know much. Not much to go on. But they knew that Marion was dead and they had known Marion in the flesh, up until yesterday itself and so that was enough to fuel conversation.

As they imagined a weirdly fictive future in which Marion wasn't around, they could go on talking. They could talk about how there would now be no smiling blonde-streaked Marion at the deli counter, putting on a fresh pair of polythene gloves. Patting lids on little plastic tubs of olives or paté. Sticking on the label with its price and weight.

Wisha wisha wisha went the scratchy paper.

He couldn't help dwelling on all of this. He was forty-two and hadn't yet known anyone who had died. It was all new to him. It gave him and Kim something to talk about.

Wisha wisha wisha.

On the staff night out last Christmas, he had even danced with Marion. Somewhere, some club, a little less trendy than last night's venue. They had been plastered and he was courageous. It had been a nostalgia night where they had played songs from the Eighties and Marion had danced close to him, breathing garlic, ginger and lager from her dinner straight up into his sweating, streaming face.

They had pressed close for Spandau Ballet. Her bloke Tony wasn't there. He was on a sales conference, away. They hadn't mentioned him. Geoff was flattered, amazed. They had swayed out of the orbit of their workmates.

Marion - who didn't really smell of the deli counter cheeses and cooked meats as Kim had often said - who smelled only of her Christmas staff night dinner and some scent - Poison, he thought it was Poison - put her hands up to his face and said he wasn't a bad-looking bloke, really. He should find himself a nice lass. She was astonished that he hadn't.

Wisha wisha wisha.

Marion had told him she was surprised he lived alone. Decent bloke like him. She had sighed heavily. Why couldn't people look beyond the surface? She was pressing her face to his shirt front. Why couldn't they get past appearances?

Wisha wisha.

He had felt his erection start to soften at this. He'd been dancing pigeon-toed, tucking his arse back as she danced against him to 'True'. He'd have died if he had brushed against her and she'd felt his todger all hard like that. But it was subsiding anyway now.

You are. You're a decent bloke.

Wisha.

Cooked meats, Geoff thought. That's not what her blonde hair had smelled of. She'd been tipsy, of course, saying stuff like that to him. Marion, drunk, swaying in his capable, freckled arms as the last song of the night finished. Rocking slightly. And then he'd realised she was sobbing gently. Marion looked up at him as the lights started to come on. Tears in her eyes, party streamers round her neck.

'Women need a bloke like you to depend on,' she told him.

He smiled, disconcerted at how close to his her face seemed to be. Looming up. Was she after a kiss? This was the time. He wasn't sure he could go through with it. It would be more hassle, after – more than it was worth. And he would have to take the responsibility and the blame.

'Not like Tony,' she said, and her face fell again.

He was rubbing her back and the material of her Christmas party dress felt rough. Cheap, he thought, and then he stopped rubbing and patting when he could suddenly feel her bra strap under his palm.

She caught his eye again and said, 'Tony lies to me. He's a car salesman, right? Sets off every morning with his mobile and his briefcase and his suit on. Gets in his car to go to work.'

Geoff's mouth was dry. He wanted to ask a question, ask if maybe she thought Tony was having an affair.

'He doesn't go to work,' Marion said.

'No?' Geoff said softly.

'There's no money coming into the account,' she said. 'There hasn't been for two months. He isn't going to work. He hasn't got a job.'

She had cracked up crying again, but there was a frightening laugh in her voice too. Like Alma Cogan, Geoff thought.

'He's pretending he's still got a job. For my sake, Geoff. He won't tell me he's lost his job. God knows where he goes instead.'

Their Christmas night out had ended soon after. Awkwardly, with Kim coming over and looking mightily annoyed at their dancing together. With the nightclub closing down, with their being the last few to leave and a confusion of punters and illegal taxis parked outside. And he had never talked again with Marion about her husband's deception. He still didn't know if it was true. Maybe he'd never know now. At least Marion would never have to worry about it or upset herself anymore.

Finished in here, anyway.

He was the type of man to take a peek at the condition of his stools, just in case. A conditioned reflex. On this occasion, though, he didn't: keen as he was to return to Kim. He washed his hands with cucumber scented soap.

On the stairs back down he resolved to talk with Kim on cheerier matters. He was sure he would think of something. Maybe he would get her onto complaining about her mother. Kim seemed to love talking like that. What ridiculous, hare-brained nonsense her old mother was up to now.

I can, Geoff thought, reaching the ground floor and taking a deep breath before re-entering the cafe bar: I can draw anyone out of themselves. You don't have to be bright. It's just a knack. Just human warmth and understanding, that's me. And sometimes ladies love that. Even if they don't say that they do.

153

6

By the time Elsa was back home with her dogs she was pretty tired out. She would have to be more careful with herself. Take more naps or something. She left the dogs in the lobby with their pals and then she realised she could hear voices in the kitchen.

Kim had brought Geoff back. They were drinking lagers straight from the can and they'd had a takeaway out of silver dishes.

Elsa brightened at the sight of them there, chatting away. The kitchen reeked of curry and they had spilled some of the greasy mess on Elsa's good cloth, clean on that morning. But they were getting on, the beggars! They were getting on fine.

As she came in, blinking under the fluorescent lighting, Geoff was scraping back his chair and standing for her.

'You're out late,' Kim said, staring at her.

'Busy day,' smiled Elsa, and motioned Geoff to sit down again. His manners were absurdly old-fashioned. 'You've been having an Indian, I see.'

'Given myself indigestion,' Geoff said. 'I always eat them too fast.'

'Those bhajis were underdone,' Kim sighed. 'They were still floury inside. Have you eaten anything, Mum?'

'Not yet. There's still some Pek ham in the fridge. I'll make a little sandwich before I pop off upstairs. Isn't this nice! All of us in the kitchen!'

Kim looked at her as if she was being ridiculous.

'It's a kind of post-work wake,' Geoff told her. 'A friend of ours has died. Kim didn't want to be alone in the house.'

'Oh.' Elsa sat down. 'Who was this?'

'I don't know how you can eat that tinned pork,' said Kim with a grimace. 'It's all that ... mechanically-retrieved meat. I've seen it on the news. It's the same for hot dogs. You know what they do, don't you? After they've taken off all the prime cuts, they hang the skeletons up in a big room, and then they send in the robots ...'

'Send in the robots!' Elsa laughed. To her, Kim looked a little bleary and serious. Elsa sang lightly, 'Isn't it rich? Aren't we a pair?'

Kim wouldn't be deterred. 'They send in these robots with loads of metal arms and hands with scalpels and things and they pluck off all the rubbish meat and scraps and bits. That's what they press into those tins, Mum. That's what you get, all squashed up together, that's what you put into your nice little sandwiches for bedtime.' Kim stopped then and looked to her mother for a reaction.

'Well, I like it,' Elsa said. 'I've eaten it all my life. It's done me no harm.'

'No?' Kim tried to draw Geoff in. He looked wary. 'You

know what she told me? What they lived off in that horrible, primitive old village she grew up in? She reckons they used to go out into the fields, pick grass, boil it up and eat it!' Kim let out a yelp of laughter. 'She used to eat grass!'

'It was a special kind of grass,' Elsa sighed. 'Like kale or something.'

'You were like savages!' Kim burst out. 'Pigs in the garden! Chickens in the house!'

'They wouldn't allow that now, would they?' Elsa said.

'Too right!' Kim said. 'God, when I think where you came from. What we've managed to escape from ...'

'You couldn't keep livestock inside your house now. No, indeed,' said Geoff.

They both looked at him. He had surprised them by butting in. But what irked Kim more was that both mother and daughter had stopped in their tracks, instinctively, just because a man had spoken up.

'No, indeed,' he burbled on. 'Not in this day and age. You know, I think it's the Dark Ages we're living in now. Honestly, I think we are. When they've got these heaps of dead cows and all that, all set alight with their hooves sticking up out of the flames. And then they're leading out the little lambs and shooting them in the head with staple guns and shoving them in pits and it's all full of disease, with lime shoved on top, and it's getting into the water system and the food chains and the smoke in the air and all ...'

'Jesus, Geoff,' said Kim.

'Well, I think it's awful,' Geoff said. 'It's like our store. That's going down the tubes as well. Who'd have thought that, eh? It's all going to hell. All of it.'

'Well!' Elsa said. 'Thanks for coming round and cheering us ladies up, Geoffrey.'

'It's everything unnatural that's caused it,' Geoff said. 'The animals. Well, they were feeding one animal to another, weren't they? All ground up so it was cannibalism. Horses eating each other. It was like doom. It's like everything unnatural.'

Kim bristled. 'I don't think my mum wants to hear any more of this gloomy talk, Geoff. She's an elderly lady.'

'I think the poor thing's upset about something,' said Elsa.

'Is he bugger.'

'I'm sorry, Mrs Rivers,' Geoff told her gently.

Actually, Elsa had rather liked the soft, thoughtful way Geoff had been talking, one hand stroking patterns in the embroidered table cloth. He had been soothing. He'd sounded almost like a minister or a priest.

'Never mind,' Elsa said. 'It was very interesting.'

'Not bad for someone who works behind a counter,' said Kim.

'You work behind a counter too, Kim,' her mother said. 'Doesn't mean you can't think about all sorts of things.'

'I do! I think about all sorts!' Kim was out of her chair and across the kitchen in a flash. 'Sometimes I think terrible things!'

There was a pause and then Geoff was tugging on his sports jacket. 'I reckon I'll head off.'

On the doorstep he called down the hall to them: 'I'm sorry if I upset you both ...'

'Yes, goodbye, Geoff,' Kim called out and listened for the door slamming.

Her mother scooted past her and up the stairs. 'You've put me right off my suppertime sandwiches, lady. And ...' She fixed her daughter with a beady gaze, gripping the banister rail. 'If you want anything at all to come out of your friendship with that good man, you're going a rotten way about it.'

Before Kim could answer back, Elsa was away. She was warbling, 'Wish Me Luck As You Wave Me Goodbye,' just so Kim couldn't get back at her.

Kim left the mess in the kitchen. She left the dogs in the lobby to fend for themselves. If her mother couldn't be bothered, then neither could she.

Kim went upstairs and saw by the hall clock that it was later than she'd thought. What on earth had her mother been doing out all that time? It wasn't a bingo night. Then she thought: Jesus. It's bingo tomorrow. She'd promised to go with her.

Kim went past her mother's door, the bathroom and her

own bedroom door. She went to the spare bedroom instead.The room prepared for guests they never really had. The one with the oldest bed, and the dressing table that had been around in their house since the Fifties. All the oldest and most worn out things were in here. Except for the computer and its accoutrements.They were only a few months old.They were giving off their steady, comforting hum.

Kim shut herself into the guest room and sat still for a while before logging on. She closed her eyes and reminded herself who she was. Someone better than this. Someone with more to say.A woman who didn't have terrible dreams and who stayed awake on purpose to keep them away. A woman who could chat, chat easily about any topic under the sun and make herself diverting, flirtatious, absolutely charming.

Kim clicked through the routine of windows, moving further and further in through the screens. She was expert. She was home.

Brazenhussy strode comfortably into the room.

7

Every week or so she'd have to take her mother to bingo. The big bingo in town. Penance. Duty.Whatever.

Eyes down, everyone.

Kim resented it, of course. She went along with her mother because she'd promised to. But she wouldn't promise to enjoy it.

159

Bingo was an insult. That's the best they could come up with? To keep everyone occupied and entertained?

Everyone hunched over in an overlit space and moving only to fetch a cup of tea or to go to the loo.

All the hectic violence of the numbers being thrown at you. You wouldn't think it complicated, but it was. All sorts of skill was needed.

The old ladies her mother sat by were intent, holding their dabbing pens only an inch or so above their books of magic numbers. Their eyes were darting about their small grids.

The dabbers dabbed and you could hear them thumping down in a concert of small triumphs, all through the hall.

The cheap sugar paper absorbed the dabbers' ink and the numbers and the wet ink fascinated Kim, making her dizzy and eventually cross.

She would never win anything. She couldn't keep up with the old ladies, and this really galled her. She cursed along with her mother when others, at other tables, called out, 'Here!', 'House!', or they gave out the altogether more common cry of, 'Bingo!'

Funny that her mother didn't know any of this lot by name. No one called out hello to her as she came into the wide room. She was here quite a lot. You'd have thought she'd have made some friends. Her mother could be altogether mysterious, if not strange.

Kim looked at her mother's tight, concentrating face and

the mass of steel wool hair tottering and wobbling as she dabbed her numbers.

Diagonals. Corners. Lines across and lines up. Other, more arcane rules and systems. The caller announced the new games and the new books with merciless ease: no time for virgins to be catching up.

You learned by trying, by chancing your arm and paying your dues. No one explained the rules.

An old cinema. Hey, in the Forties we used to come here, her mother had once told her, startlingly. You could hardly see the screen for all the cigarette smoke. Purple and blue, like magic. Joan Crawford and Katherine Hepburn, Cary Grant and Errol Flynn.

And the fun what we got up to here! You would sit through programme after programme if no one noticed, and you could stay here all day and all night. Newsreels and ice cream. We learned all about the world from here. And we didn't have to go nowhere else.

It was too bright now. All candy-coloured inside, pinks and lime greens. Kim's mother didn't complain though, about things going to the bad.

When she thought about it, it was true: Elsa never really did complain about things going to the bad.

'It was all shabby curtains before,' she told Kim during a lull. 'It was smelly and a bit seedy, truth be told. Well, it's not like that now, is it?'

'Clean as a shopping mall. Clean as the Disney shop.'

'Ee, if your dad could see it. He really would think he was in a different world. Even bingo's not the same. Even that's cleaner. He'd be so shocked, your dad.'

'He would.'

'So even if he hadn't gone on to the next life ... he'd still think he had, if he came here.'

'That's true.'

They didn't have the ball machine anymore, jiggling its bright coloured balls and spitting them out - ping, pong, ping - with their numbers painted on. All that had gone. The bingo caller was no longer some smarmy fella in a black tuxedo and he wasn't wearing white, starchy gloves and gently popping the new balls into a clear, plastic brain.

That was all gone as well and, actually, Elsa missed that bit: watching his fastidious face and hands as he plucked the numbered balls out of the chute at the bottom of the brain.

Nowadays the numbers came up on TV screens all over the shop. That was a lot better. Especially for those who used to have to squint.

'Are you sweating yet?' Elsa asked Kim.

That's what they all used to ask. That's what you used to have to ask, whenever your neighbour looked like she was coming close to a full house.

'Are you sweating yet? Ee, these books we've got this week are rubbish, our Kim. They're worse than them last week. We're hardly getting a single number ...'

Kim nodded grimly, eyes down again. She hated the mention of sweating.

Her mother went on, 'Still, it's a whole night's entertainment ... and it isn't really gambling ...'

'If Dad's really in heaven,' Kim said, 'you'd think he would at least use his influence.'

'What are you saying?'

'If he's really in the afterlife, he could at least find some way to give us a win ...'

Actually, Kim wasn't too far away from a win. With a shock, she saw it was only one number she needed. She couldn't believe it. Sweat pricked up.

But some kind of fault had developed. The TV screens flickered, buzzed, flickered again.

'Ladies and gentlemen. There is an electrical hitch ... Please be patient for the next numbers...'

Kim crossed her fingers, waiting on this last one. 'Come on, Dad ...'

Her mother hadn't noticed how tense she was.

Come on, come on, Dad. Give us the number.

When the TV screens flickered back on and revealed the number, they all said number twenty-five.

Which was just what Kim needed.

'House!' And her mother picked up the cry delightedly. They had a deal to split all winnings between them, and so now both of them were shouting.

They had won one hundred and sixty-five pounds.

They were no kind of addicts. It wasn't like some casino. Mother and daughter knew to quit while they were ahead.

They took their money and left in triumph. Chips reeking with vinegar on the way out.

'That was Dad who did that,' Kim said. 'He was helping us. He brought that twenty-five out.'

'It could be.'

On the bus home, Kim had a terrible thought.

What if she had tempted him out of the afterlife, where he'd been happy, having a RIP-roaring time, and what if she'd drawn him back to the earth? What if he couldn't get back now? And all for the sake of less than two hundred quid?

A soul in purgatory forever now, she thought gloomily. This is how your average hauntings begin.

She had got her dad to fix it. Like the good old fix-it he always was. Mum was too busy. He was swabbing scabbed knees. Poking dolls' eyes back in their heads. Sorting out the fights she got into with kids down their street.

If Dad's stuck here now, he'll be watching, she thought. He'll look at Mum and me on the back seat of the bus, shunting along home with our chips and our easy money.

What's he going to think?

He might take a good long look at my life, Kim thought. He will know all the secret stuff.

He'll be like a cloud of something, seeping under doors.

Outside the light was spangly – bright coins of yellow and green, turning the window panes opaque. For the rest of the journey Kim thought of her invisible, uncontainable dad.

All the rest of us are collections of organs. A loose, jumbled, baggy set of organs, all contained. We're like carrierbags of blood.

Without those bags, that skin, if it's all set free, what are we converted into? Numbers. Electricity. Magical impulses. Radio waves and words and radiation. Spirit and soul.

Like alcohol in a cocktail. You can't see it's there, but you can taste it and if you sniff it you can smell it and it's there.

Or he's a set of random emotions. And is it possible to control your emotions if you've got no body to put them in? Is that why spirits can seem so malign sometimes?

Shut up, Kim, she told herself.

Dad would always make sure he's doing things for the best.

One hundred and sixty-five quid!

Not too bad!

8

The buzz off the bingo winnings didn't last long.

Her mother had gone off to whisper sweet nothings to old Mr Pastry in the hospice and Kim was determined not to be left in the house by herself. Work again tomorrow morning and if she didn't get out now and do something, and make something of Sunday night, she'd be wasting her time.

So she decided to get herself round Marion's house.

She felt bad for not thinking much about Marion this weekend. Only when Geoff had prompted her. Now, on Sunday night, it settled in again that deli counter Marion was dead and there were deep commiserations to offer and condolences (that was the right word) and arrangements to find out about.

She'd have to get her good black coat cleaned. So she needed to know when the funeral was, to make sure she had time for the dry cleaner's.

Kim knew where Marion had lived with Tony, because once they'd had a little, unsuccessful soirée for a few select work mates from the store. Kim remembered waiting in their front room for a taxi, the last one to leave, though she'd have preferred to have gone earlier. She could see that Marion and Tony were eager to get to bed.

Actually, at the time, she'd been a bit perturbed. Tony had been talking about importing his cars and his rich collectors and she hadn't been very interested. He was just mouthy. But still he'd kept on talking, rolling his shirt sleeves up, all animated on the syrupy Chianti they were drinking and Kim had been frightened that Marion's husband was coming onto her.

By then Marion had been going round with a black bin bag, picking up the cans and the paper plates, emptying the ash trays and she hadn't seemed to have minded that Tony was chatting away to Kim, and touching her bare shoulder and looking into her eyes like that.

And Kim had started to fret that the two of them were swingers and this was all some kind of seduction. They'd started out with the express intention of having a swinging party and all the other guests had fled and Kim was the one the two of them had designs on.

But then her taxi had bleated out in the roadway and she never could quite be sure.

She knew where they lived, anyway. In a row of houses at the back of Sainsburys. Not quite the rough end of town, but on its way.

The sun was going down, at last, on the whole weekend, as she composed her face, smoothed down her blouse and jacket lapels, and rapped neatly on their front door.

A young woman answered it almost immediately.

'Oh!' said Kim.

'Yes?' The young woman had dyed black hair, the type that looked synthetic and unwashed in a certain kind of light.

167

She was in a navy skirt and blouse, quite smart, and her chin was thrust forward aggressively.

Kim gathered herself up, and hid her surprise. 'I've come to offer my condolences,' she said. 'For Marion. I was a valued colleague of hers.'

The young woman with the jet black hair was looking Kim up and down and suddenly Kim realised that she ought to have brought something with her. Flowers, or a card with flowers on, expressing her deepest sympathy. But where could she lay her hands on such things on a Sunday night?

'You'd better come in,' the young woman sighed. She opened the door and Kim stepped in. 'I'm Clare,' she said wearily, as if that explained everything.

In the living room Tony looked up at Kim with blotchy, uncomprehending eyes.

Kim was beginning to wish she'd never bothered.

'Tony,' she said warmly. 'I'm so, so sorry to hear your news.'

'Oh.'

'Kim,' she told him. 'Remember? Kim who worked with Marion at the store.'

'Oh, yes,' he said, still not moving off the settee. Ay, she thought. Remember, the one who you were telling all about your work? The same one you were getting all touchy-feely with that time, on that selfsame settee. God, men were so faithless.

'I was there on Friday night,' she prompted. 'I was sat right next to you in the noodle bar.'

'Of course.'

But on Friday night, even before the tragedy had occurred and anyone got wind of it, he hadn't really been part of it all, Kim thought. He'd still looked like he hated being there, amongst them all.

Oh come on, Kim, she told herself sternly, stop being so awful. The man is in grief.

At last Tony stood up, hitching his pants.

'This is Marion's daughter ... Clare,' he explained.

Kim turned to the young woman with new interest. You'd never have guessed. She looked nothing like her. Kim told her, 'Your mother was a wonderful woman.'

'Oh?'

What's the matter with the pair of them? Kim wondered. You'd think they'd never been in decent company before.

'You're the only one to come round and say so,' said Clare. 'So much for all her great work mates. Do you want a brew? I've just put the kettle on.'

Kim nodded, blushing slightly at what she'd taken as a compliment.

Tony followed them through to the kitchen. Kim was looking with interest at the mess. There were bulging bags and cases laying about, as if Clare had just arrived. You could tell no one had been round with a hoover for days.

'Clare's come all the way down from Glasgow,' Tony said.

'That's a long trip,' said Kim.

Clare was at work in the kitchen, opening cupboards, looking for cups and saucers, sugar and spoons. 'I'm worn out. They had works on the line and they laid on a coach from Peterborough. It was like a nightmare.'

'Oh, it's awful when they do that,' Kim said. 'It's like you're coming to the back of beyond, isn't it?'

'And then it was a taxi from Ely. I had to share it with three people I'd never seen before in my life. And they all wanted to chat and act like it was a great adventure. Well, I wasn't in the mood and I told them. I sat next to the cab driver and kept my mouth shut.' She filled the teapot with water that had gone off the boil.

'So you've had an awful journey,' said Kim brightly. 'And what a thing to come down for! Poor you.' She watched Clare shrug self-deprecatingly.

'Really,' Kim went on, 'it's a shame you couldn't have made it while your mother was still alive.'

Oops. Now she wanted to bite her own tongue off.

'What's that supposed to mean?' Clare flashed.

'Nothing ... it, it just came out wrong.'

Tony said, 'I think she just meant that ...'

Clare snapped, 'I don't need any help from you, thanks.'

'All I was saying,' Kim said, 'was that I'm sure your poor mother wouldn't have wanted to see you struggle down from Glasgow in such sad circumstances. She would have liked to have been here ...'

'Don't tell me what my mother would have wanted.'

Clare was poking a spoon into the teapot, mashing the leaves.

There was a very awkward pause.

'Kim's just trying to be nice, Clare,' said Tony.

Clare snorted and poured the tea out, quickly. Clods of tealeaves were coming out as well, swirling in the china cups. She'd forgotten the strainer. She said: 'I wish I'd come down earlier, too.' Her voice sounded very much younger, all of a sudden, tight and high. 'I wish I'd seen her alive.' She turned to Kim and Kim's heart relented towards her, she looked so hurt. 'We'd been fighting for a couple of years now, you see. Every time we got together, there'd be some kind of to-do. We couldn't help it. She'd start picking fault with me, my life, all my choices. She'd be picking away and criticizing and I'd just flip. She drove me crazy. Here's your tea.'

'Mothers can be impossible,' Kim agreed. 'I've lived with mine all my life. Or rather, she's lived with me all mine.'

'Really?' said Clare.

'She's a funny old bird,' said Kim and, saying it, she felt awful. It was an awful thing to say about her mother.

'Then you must get on well,' said Clare. 'You're very lucky, then.'

'I suppose so. We were out at the bingo together just this afternoon. We won one hundred and sixty-five pounds.'

'Oh. Good.'

Tony had drifted away again, into the living room, leaving the women to it.

'The funeral's on Friday,' said Clare. 'I'm taking over arrangements. I'll need your help, Kim. I don't know the people she worked with. You'll have to help me.'

'I'd be very glad to.' Kim glowed with pride. Suddenly Clare was talking to her like someone valuable, in the centre of it all.

'Was it you who went with Tony to the scene of the accident?' Clare asked. 'He was on about a colleague of Mum's who went to the hospital and stayed with him, looked after him and everything...'

For a second Kim almost said yes, it was her. But that was the kind of lie it was easy to be caught out in. 'No,' she said, 'that was Glenda.'

'Oh, yes. Glenda,' said Clare as she led them to sit at the pine table in the breakfast room. She moved her handbag off a chair for Kim, and shoved a pile of newspaper supplements away so they could set their cups down.

Clare was really acting like she owned the place and had a right to, Kim thought. She was amazed at the young woman's confidence. Best china out, too, just for an ordinary cup of tea. But she supposed that death was one of those special times and you couldn't really use mugs.

'Glenda,' said Kim, and couldn't help herself grimacing at the name, 'she was a supervisor at work. She's just retired.'

'Oh,' said Clare. 'I thought it would have been you, somehow. Probably because you're the only one who's bothered coming round today.'

Kim smiled, pleased. 'Glenda's not been round today?'

'Apparently not. Maybe because Tony told her I was coming.'

'Ah.'

'I don't know what that's about,' Clare tutted. 'Ever since I've got here it's been Glenda this and Glenda that. Tony going on about how Glenda saved his life and how he'd never have got through any of it without Glenda. Well, I've started thinking Glenda's a bloody marvel. I've started thinking all sorts of things.'

'Really?'

Clare scowled. 'Glenda helped him get over it, he says! Well, I wanted to laugh. I wanted to ask him, What, are you over it already, Tony? Not even two days later? I wish I bloody was.'

'Quite,' said Kim.

'Whoever this Glenda is, she must be a bloody miracle worker.'

'Well,' said Kim thoughtfully. 'She's no slouch.'

Clare darted her a look. 'What do you mean?'

'I suppose I mean, she's quick on the uptake.'

Clare's face had gone pale. Then she asked in a lower voice, 'Is she his fancy woman?'

Kim was shocked. 'I'm sure I don't know.'

'The way he was going on about her, soon as I arrived, that was the first thing that sprang into my mind. Precious Glenda, I thought - the bugger's been carrying on behind Mum's back the whole time. Now she's dead and he's free to do what he wants with Glenda. Glenda was round straight away, helping him out. Well, no bloody wonder. I bet she was bloody helpful.'

Kim was thrilled. 'I'm sure it isn't true.'

'Huh,' said Clare. 'I know Tony.'

Kim frowned. 'I take it he's not your natural father?'

'Too right. If I had his genes in me I'd slash my wrists. He's one of the reasons Mum and I fell out. She married that fat bugger and I couldn't stick him. And she made her choice - husband over daughter. We never got over that.'

174

'Oh, that's so sad!' said Kim. 'Because I've always thought that a parent's first loyalty was to their children. Over and above themselves.'

'You'd think so, wouldn't you?'

Kim stared at the open door that led to the living room. 'Well, I'm certainly seeing Tony in a new light.'

'He goes on like Mr Perfect,' said Clare. 'Smarming round all the women.'

'Ay, he does.'

'And no one can see the harm in him, because he knows all the patter. He's very smooth. That's how he sells cars. Mum was daft. She couldn't see through him. I could, though. Now he's got this Glenda in his pocket.'

Kim swirled her tea, making the leaves whirlpool. 'Well ...'

'It's like something you read about in the Sunday papers,' Clare said. 'Moving some old tart in, soon as Mum's dead. Before she's even cold. I'll bet he's been waiting for this bloody moment.'

'You read of all sorts going on,' Kim said.

'I always thought he was two-faced. That he had some secret agenda going on. He didn't think anything of Mum, not really.'

Kim thought Clare was talking too loudly.

'There's no will, you know,' Clare said. 'I asked him straight out.'

'I'd have thought Marion would have done one out,' Kim said. 'For the peace of mind. She was such a sensible woman.'

'Well, he says there's no will. That's what he says.'

'Oh.'

'I think there's going to be ructions,' sighed Clare. 'I've got a feeling. I mean, I'm not greedy, but I can't believe Mum would go without ... leaving provisions.'

'No, she wouldn't.'

'I might have a fight on my hands,' said Clare. 'He had all of her while she was alive. He squeezed me right out of the picture. Well, not now. I'm her natural daughter.'

'Of course you are.'

Clare looked Kim dead in the eye. 'I'm glad you came round. There's no one I can talk to about this. It's reassuring to find out that at least Mum had a good friend here.'

Kim smiled at this. 'I tried to be. I really tried, Clare, love.'

Elsa Rivers

Elsa and her daughter live together. They have lived together for all of Kim's life. There are no secrets in this house, at least as far as Elsa is concerned. They are a family unit – that's the terminology – and they look out for each other. They take their holidays and breaks with each other, they have their meals together, they discuss their days and they go to bingo as mother and daughter. They don't always get on, but overall their relationship is a good one. Each would fight tooth and nail for the other.

On Tuesday tea-time Elsa returns from her doctor's surgery and she's very calm. Before her appointment she popped into the town hall to enquire after a special marriage licence and about that, as well, she's very calm. The results of the two visits she's paid today have made her very calm. They were painless, almost easy. And all of this is secret from Kim. Kim knows nothing about any of these developments.

Elsa fills the kettle and her heart beats a merry tattoo. She goes out to the lobby to feed her dogs (little biscuits with cheese grated on top, because they like it so much) and she strokes them, stooped over in the cool, musty lobby. She feels a strange satisfaction.

I'm the woman, the old woman, doing small, ordinary teatime chores and I'm the woman with secrets. I've got a secret fiance and I'm planning a gunshot wedding. And really, a gunshot wedding was absurdly easy to arrange. It was all going through. Friday would be the day. She would sort it out somehow. Kim had no idea about that yet. She would have to be told. Goodness knows what her reaction would be.

My daughter is so fiery.

But in the meantime it was delicious.

And I am the woman who took herself under her own steam to her own GP and confessed all. I told him all my covered-up fears. I let him examine me.

He was so, so young. This blue blush of beard on his cheeks and chin. A dark, smudgey-eyed, concerned doctor, so careful with me. I watched his face through the whole examination. His cool fingers. His dark eyes widened as he felt, as his fingers came across what I've been feeling a full year now, through its slow and steady growth. The white showed around his eyes and he looked at me.

He stepped back, went to wash his hands efficiently at his neat little sink. He told me in careful, measured tones, that he knew that I knew that the hospital would have to see me. And as soon as possible. And I nodded. There was nothing much more he could tell me. At that moment we were both equals. It's not what I expected. That quiet between us. It was like respect, almost. It was quiet. We were both in possession of the facts.

******

The snow had fled by the end of the morning.

Now it was spring, apparently, and people were starting to

178

sit out in Chapelfield Gardens for the afternoon. Only a week ago there had been hectic rain and then there was last night's surprising, late night snow. For months the grass had looked water-logged and you didn't want to hang around too much. You wanted to be at home, looking out at the dreary day with your heating on.

Elsa tended to take her dogs out no matter what the weather. On recent Saturdays she had been here virtually by herself in the small town park, perched on a bench by the bandstand, watching the dogs run around. In a way she preferred that, setting them free to investigate and rummage around in the hedgerows where they wanted. But now there were people, rashly over-estimating the warmth of the March sun, in their t-shirts and little tops, bringing their children out, content to dawdle.

There were crocuses out, lilac and white and miraculous. Dwarfish, peeved daffodils sat in drying clumps. She hoped her dogs wouldn't cause any bother. She could only manage to walk two of her pets at a time and this afternoon it was George the Shitzu and Gracie, the rollicking Border Collie. She steered them away from the flower beds and the smaller children. She wouldn't want anyone getting an accidental nip, but she was also, secretly, thinking that parents (especially the younger ones) ought to keep a keener eye on their offspring. They should take some responsibility too.

Honestly, some of the parents were even lying out on the grass, letting their toddlers do what they wanted. And surely it was madness to lie on the grass after a night of snow? They were people who'd grown up in a time since all the seasons went haywire. No wonder they had no sense.

Elsa steered and controlled her dogs with a surprising strength. She was all of four feet tall. She looked bigger because of the way she kept her hair piled up. She was very proud of her hair. Her daughter Kim kept telling her to have it all cut off. She kept suggesting that her mother have a nice, easy-to-care-for perm. Get it shampooed and set once a week and never have to bother.

As if having a mother with yards of luxurious hair was some kind of embarrassment to her!

Kim seemed to think that perms were every woman's destiny. She'd been having them herself since she was thirteen. Elsa Rivers considered that her daughter had ruined her own god-given hair with bleach and perming solutions. But that was Kim for you. Always so sure that she knew best.

Then Elsa started thinking about Kim being out till all hours and staying up so much of the night. Out with that nice Geoff, who saw her to the door every time. Wouldn't it be something if they could settle down together? And leave the old mother to have some peace on her own?

But, deep down, Elsa Rivers knew that Kim didn't really think much of her hearty, sloppy, ginger work colleague. Kim was stringing him along for the company and the convenience. Just as she had with other men through the years.

Actually, there was still a nip in the air. As the afternoon went on, it wasn't keeping the warmth. Elsa thought about heading back with the dogs and that was when she saw young Darren coming out of the police station with a friend.

The station was all red brick and smoked glass, bang between the theatre and the small park. Darren was tired-looking, tousled, his short, fair hair sticking up. He looked thoughtful and rueful and as if he was waiting for his taller, darker friend to say something. They were dithering on the doorstep, as if figuring out where to go next.

Elsa took a tight grip on her dogs' leads and set her steps firmly in the boys' direction. She was thoroughly intrigued, her mouth set in a grim line. Surely Darren hadn't got himself locked up in a police cell all night! That would be something. She wouldn't have believed it of him and her mind set to ticking over what he might have done.

Whatever it was, it was the other lad at the root of it, who-ever he was. Darren was soft-hearted, she thought, and quite probably easily-led. It would be that other, cockier-looking one who had led him astray.

And then Elsa thought: Ee, if the university gets wind of Darren's being locked in a police cell, what will happen with his job? Would they get rid of him? Would he have to leave in shame? Darren had been a junior lecturer there for only a couple of years. She knew he was new to it all and still in what they called his probationary period. He was her advisor (Him at twenty whatever he was and she at seventy-seven!) and her tutor on her Twentieth Century Fiction course. She was supposed to be writing a paper for him, or part of one, this very weekend. Actually, she quite liked having an official adviser some fifty years her junior. It allowed her to become a little hapless and reckless whenever she was on campus. She could pretend that she didn't know things, either academic or administrative. She could pretend to be baffled by the masses of documenta-

181

tion and form-filling that Higher Education seemed to entail.

It was good to get the chance to sit in someone's narrow office with its breeze-blocked walls and grey carpet and have them explain things to you, oh-so-carefully. It was nice to have them looking so concerned about your not understanding this rather shocking, experimental novel you were supposed to write about for part of your degree. As if this rather shocking, experimental novel were the most important thing in the world! And that your having to understand it, to appreciate it and – what's more – to deconstruct it, were even more important than that!

It was delightful and it made Elsa smile, the earnestness of it all and the way Darren carried on. He was so keen to make sure she was all right and that she was keeping up. She was the only septugenarian sophomore in a brutal concrete building that swarmed with surly, middle class eighteen-year-olds.

They had first met in the corridor outside his office, the first day of her first year, when she was talking to the department's secretary (an alarming person who didn't appear to care who overheard the things she said). Elsa had been explaining that her daughter had almost pushed her into a semi-permanent. 'She wanted me to have a new perm for the new term!'

Elsa had been shouting down the corridor. Then the department's secretary was shouting back, 'But they don't even call them terms anymore. They call them semesters. Though what the fucking difference is, no one knows. They don't know jackshit round here.'

Elsa gathered that the department's secretary was an American lady. She enjoyed quilting and, as the semester went on, Elsa had shown her a number of websites from which to download new patterns and the department's secretary had given Elsa the low-down on the faculty. When Elsa told her who her advisor was, the department's secretary had approved. 'But some of the others are real assholes. I could tell you tales that would make your hair stand on end.'

Elsa had already noted that the department's secretary had also managed to avoid having a perm. And her a mature lady, too. Perhaps between them they might start a trend.

Now Elsa was hurrying up to her advisor Darren outside the police station and her dogs were sniffing busily around both the boys' feet.

'Nothing nasty, I hope?' she asked him, after they had greeted one another. Darren seemed a little flustered at seeing her and his friend was glowering at her as they were introduced.

Darren pulled a worried faced. 'Fairly nasty, Elsa. We were witnesses. Kind of. We saw the ... aftermath of a car accident.'

Her eyes lit up and she bit her bottom lip as he explained a bit more. The old lady with the impatient dogs expressed her commiserations that the boys had had to come across such a grisly thing.

'You never used to hear of so many disasters and terrible things back in the old days,' she tutted. 'Mind, you didn't hear much about anything at all, back then.'

She noticed that Darren's friend, the dark-haired boy, was crouching down now and he was petting and fussing around George and Gracie. She thought that was just a touch impolite, to exempt himself from the human conversation, and to resort to the animals. But, she reminded herself, that was just what some people were like, Elsa Rivers! People are all different to each other and you have got no right to judge, have you? This was the mantra she kept up more often than not, these days. It ran through her head like a war-time song or a show tune. Ever since she had become an honours degree student (as she proudly thought of herself) she had maintained a deliberate effort at tolerance for all types of people and behaviours.

She looked into Darren's face and he was watching the other boy, too.

Aha, she thought. That's how it is. This other one is Darren's little boyfriend. Well, it wasn't up to her to interfere. She rather liked the way her young mentor looked at his friend, all concerned. And it was no surprise to her that Darren was that way inclined.

Now came the awkward part of the conversation, when they would have to sort out how they were going to finish it and say goodbye politely and move away. Elsa knew Darren was awkward with that sort of business. When she had tutorials with him in his small office on campus, their meetings would peter out. She would suddenly be aware that he had finished and had told her everything he wanted or needed to. And now he was waiting for her to elect to go, to offer to go. He wasn't about to tell her. He wasn't about to give any heavy-handed hint that it was time she shuffled along.

'I've taken up far too much of your time,' she would protest, folding her papers up and popping them into her handbag. This would touch him, because most students had folders and plastic wallets and heaven knew what else to keep their important papers pristine and flat inside. Mrs Rivers would fold hers up like shopping lists, like bills to pay, like old birthday cards with addresses written on. She would poke them into the bottom of a bag that smelled of face powder, caked in the bottom corners.

'Oh, no,' Darren would say, flustered and alarmed that he must have looked bored, to make her want to shoot off like this. 'Not at all.' Yet he would look relieved too, that she had taken the responsibility off him.

'You'll have a whole queue of other clueless students outside! Others just like me!' She would laugh, getting up stiffly and patting her pockets. 'They'll all be wanting your help.'

At this he would look pained and worried. Really, she thought, he was too shy to be doing the job he was doing.

Now, outside the police station, Elsa Rivers knew that the onus to end this little meeting was on her again. Out here, they were just two acquaintances in ordinary life and she was the senior. Someone with a lifetime of good manners behind her.

But what came out of her mouth at that point astonished her.

'I'm coming to see you on Monday at work,' she said. 'As my advisor. Is ten o'clock all right?'

He nodded, looking surprised. 'Is it about your coursework?'

'Bless you, no,' she laughed. 'It's personal.'

'Oh,' he said.

Elsa paused, hardly believing what she was saying. 'It's something I've not told anyone else. It's a bit of a problem ... that might interfere with my university course. I don't know. I've just decided to tell you about it ... as my advisor.'

Darren looked a little green around the gills.

She took his hand and patted it. 'Don't you worry about it,' she said. 'It probably isn't anything. It's just something I haven't even told my daughter yet.'

****

Mr Pastry wasn't in the Sheltered Housing anymore.

In the end, he'd liked it in there. He'd started to like it in there just that bit too late. Now he was out of there he would think about all of the advantages to the Sheltered. They had really tried to make it like home. They'd let him do up his room just how he wanted, with his nick-nacks and his pictures and so on. And there'd been company. All those daft old women. Reasonable grounds to take a little stroll in.

All the women had known him by name.

This place wasn't as good. It wasn't meant to be. It had a

different function. But he wouldn't be here long anyway. That was the understanding.

Maybe he could break out. Maybe one night he could slip out of the main gates and under the floodlights. Then he'd be tootling off down the Unthank Road – condemned man on the run – back to the Sheltered. Back to his old, homely room.

He didn't have the heart to ask Elsa Rivers whether they'd given away his room. He knew they would have, by now. He had his retirement clock with him, and a few framed photos. Those things had come with him and stood on his white bedside table. But what had happened to the rest? Cold storage or chucked out?

Funny, the whole business. As your body shrinks up and you can do less, move less, the Authorities step in and shrink all your assets for you, too. Chaffing them off so you're easier to manage and to parcel away. Smaller and smaller till there's just a bit of you left.

'Do you know that my daughter thinks that we're romantically involved?'

'Ha!'

'Mind, she'd rather spend her time thinking about my love life than her own,' Elsa Rivers added, poking her hand down into the box of Roses she'd brought, scrabbling around at the bottom. 'They're doing new flavours of Roses chocolates,' she said thoughtfully, studying the little chart on the lid flaps. 'This one's apricot flavour, look.'

'Apricot!' Mr Pastry smiled, looking surprised.

'It's all gone exotic these days,' said Elsa. 'Well, you've not been in Sainsburys for a while, I know, but if you did, you'd not know where you were. I was looking at the fruit and vegetables and I was lost. There were things there I wouldn't dream of eating.'

Mr Pastry chuckled.

'I'm sorry I brought you chocolates with hard bits in. I should have thought.'

'Bits of nut getting under my palate,' he said. 'Can't be doing with it. I shouldn't have chocolate at all.'

'It doesn't seem fair. If there's any time you should be allowed to have whatever you want, it's now.'

'When I'm about to peg out?'

Elsa came up in an immediate blush.

'Never mind, Elsa,' he said. 'I know what's happening to me.'

She looked at him. She fixed on his huge bushy eyebrows and his luxurious white side whiskers. She tried not to look at all the medical paraphenalia: the clean-looking tubes, the tall hatstand thing with the bag hanging off it.

'I wish they'd let you bring your dogs in,' he said. 'I would have liked to see them.'

'It seems cruel not to,' she said.

It was late in the evening and the hospice staff had already bent the rules by letting Elsa visit so late. But they understood. She'd had a full early evening at the Sheltered, taking her dogs to visit their other friends. Now the dogs were tied outside. They'd be as tired as Elsa was. They'd had trembling, crepey hands patting them, conferring warmth and love.

'You do a good job with them pets of yours, Elsa,' Mr Pastry said. 'Some of that lot forget what it's like to touch another living being. No grandchildren, no visitors. When they feel another pulse, it's just someone bed-bathing them or some-such ...'

She nodded. 'People need to let their love out. Just a touch. You can starve without it. Just like you can without food.' She looked thoughtful. 'The dogs are the only company I get as well, you know. Kim's never kissed or hugged her poor old mum. Not in years. Not even when her dad died. She couldn't.'

'Ah,' he said.

'And she told me back then – we'd flared up into one of our usual rows – that she didn't recognise me as her mother. She'd look at me and not even feel related to me. I was like an alien to her.'

'That's awful, Elsa.'

'She was having a hard time. She was always her daddy's girl.'

'Yes, but to say that she didn't recognise you, wouldn't kiss you ...'

'Kim's forever holding people away. It's just how she is.'

189

'It's a different world we brung them kids into,' Mr Pastry said. 'Different to the one we knew. Isn't it? Maybe we were foolish to do it, not knowing what the world would be like. But it changed out of all recognition and we dumped our kids into it to sort it out. Or not. But when did it all change, Elsa? I mean, absolutely nothing is the same. Nothing.'

'It was life in the raw, wasn't it?' she laughed. 'Back then.'

She knew he was tempting her back. Getting her to talk about years ago. She knew he was doing it on purpose, edging the talk around.

'Ay,' he said. 'It was.' He pronounced it 'war', his Norfolk accent stronger as he thought back.

They had grown up in the same village, twenty miles out of Norwich. They had known each other then, at the same C of E village school and hadn't seen each other since war broke out. Yet Elsa had known him, the first time she'd seen him, as she was struggling into the Sheltered's lounge with her visiting dogs.

Boy Harold, he'd been back then. A second cousin of hers, something like that. Here, they called him Mr Pastry, on account of his cold hands. It had seemed too late for them to go calling each other Girl Elsa and Boy Harold, like everyone used to in those days.

'We called each other daft things, when you think on it,' he said. 'I used to call mum "Girl Mum"!' He laughed again. 'Hey, she was a terror, wasn't she? Causing all them rows. We had to move house because on them rows she had.'

'She used to take in the washing for everyone, miles

190

around,' Elsa said. 'I remember carrying ours, all wrapped in a bundle. She had those huge thick arms on her.'

'There was no running water. My grandad wouldn't have it brung in the house, even when it was offered. He had a tap put in the back garden and poor old Girl Mum used to go out with two buckets again and again, lugging them back. Heating them on the range. Scrubbing through everyone's sheets and what have you ...'

Elsa said, 'I remember sitting there with my mum and your sisters and your mother would be scrubbing and she'd be talking away a blue streak. Doing all the old stories ...'

'Ay, she were a gossip all right.'

'Well, we didn't even have radio, did we? We had to go to old Mrs Taylor's for the radio if there were owt important we needed to hear.'

'Otherwise it were just talking and gossip and causing trouble.'

'Hours listening,' she smiled.

'When do they do that now?' he asked. 'Do people still sit for hours? I can't see how they get time.'

'Life speeds up,' she said. 'Mine did. I think it did for everyone.'

He nodded stiffly and then he had to tell her he was tired. She would have to go now. He'd held out as long as he could.

She held and patted his cold long hands and she felt his fingers curl and stroke her palms.

'We should talk more about all the old days,' she said. 'I've forgotten most on it. You bring it all back to me.'

'Do I?' he whistled between his too straight, perfect teeth. 'I don't reckon I've forgotten anything. It's all still here somewhere.'

'Good.'

'You give me someone to tell it to. You know it's real. That I'm not just delirious, talking nonsense.'

'I know it's real,' she nodded.

'There aren't many of us left, are there? I reckon we're the last, don't you?'

'I reckon so, Boy Harold.'

'All that matters is what's real, isn't it? What we knew was real. When we go ... all those people, all what went on then ... that all goes, don't it? It all vanishes then. It just blinks out.'

She nodded and gave the back of his hand one last pat. 'Yes, it does.'

'I can't bear that,' he said. 'I can put up with pegging out, I think. I've come to the end and I'm not sad about that. It's all mapped out for you, I think. But I can't bear it ... that all them gone by and all what they were ... fading out like that, forever. Like they needn't have existed. I don't want to be the last one here, Elsa. It's too much.'

'I'm still around and about, Boy Harold.'

******

Heaven is a disaster.

It isn't what you were expecting and it doesn't live up to all that. You thought you'd had it all mapped out, the geography of the place you'd like to be and that one day you'd open your eyes and it would all be true.

Elsa Rivers had watched her husband, Frank – oh, years ago, when furniture was heavy and lasted a lifetime – she'd watched him draw detailed aerial plans for their house and where everything would go.

She, the dutiful wife, would widen her eyes at the number of bedrooms he'd set aside for children. Nursery after nursery on the landings in the too-big home they'd bought. Her eyes had widened as she peeped over Frank's shoulder but she hadn't said anything. She'd just watched him plot and draw, plot and draw, on large sheets of paper, where everything would go.

And it had. The heavy furniture was still to this day in those places; the tallboys and beds and mothbally wardrobes. They were there even now with him dead so long. No hope of a tiny woman like Elsa moving such things by herself.

Was heaven a disaster, Frank? When you got there, did it disappoint?

He'd known it in some detail, and had described it to her, the long nights they'd sat together, while he was dying. He had subscribed to the view that it would simply be as he expected. All the things he wanted, arranged just so.

It was as if he had a contract in his hand and could be depended upon to sue.

When he'd passed on, Elsa had fretted about this.

She imagined him kicking up a storm. Wanting his money back. Not his life, of course. Frank, more practical than most, wouldn't have expected that kind of refund.

Elsa thought heaven would be just like Stansted airport. She had been there only once, flying to Italy with Kim a couple of summers ago. But she had known, as soon as she saw the place: this is what heaven was like.

Smoked glass and dove grey carpets. Smaller versions of the shops and restaurant chains you knew from home. People queueing anxiously with all their necessaries strapped up.

It was the kind of arrangement of people and belongings that people must want. Because this was what had been settled on. Because Stansted had been evolved like this and people chose to spend so much of their time in airports like this. It seemed plain to Elsa that heaven must be like that too. Efficient at putting lots of people in transit, and at their ease. You'd always be on the move there, she thought.

Talking to Mr Pastry last night had put these thoughts in her mind.

After a sensible breakfast of Weetabix with warm milk – mashing them into a fibrous, frothy paste – she called up the stairs to Kim and reminded her about bingo this afternoon.

Kim still wasn't sleeping through the night. More often then not she was in the spare room, on that damned computer. Elsa could see the midnight oil burning from her bed, the glow creeping under ill-fitting doors down the hall. She could hear the computer chime out each time Kim clicked the wrong button.

It was a severe master, that computer. At least, by the sounds of it. Elsa was no expert. Though she knew that tinkling, musical noise, that cheery fanfare it gave when you turned it on was all just a put-on. The computer would freeze or damage its own memory if you did the wrong things to it. Elsa had seen her daughter tear her own hair with frustration at the things that computer could do. It sat there like an invalid.

Elsa spooned up the last of her Weetabix and decided that Kim treated that machine as if it were her lover. She lavished all those hours on it. She clicked the spare bedroom door closed and stayed there with it all that time. It wasn't a healthy existence for the girl.

Still, her old mum was here to rescue her. To pull her out of herself. To make her get out and breathe God's good air. To make her enjoy herself in the real world ...

****

'I thought you were a wild boy. I always did.'

'That's what you thought?'

'Ay, I did, Boy Harold. Remember, you used to lead all us kids through the woods, where we weren't supposed to go.'

'I did. I remember that. I was fearless.'

'All the kids in the village running after you. You were the king of the kids.'

He chuckled. 'I was. Everyone would do as I said.'

'We ran wild. We were in awe of you. We ran through the woods, all where we weren't supposed to go, at the back of Lord Rothermere's estate, all his land ...'

Elsa looked at the old man, dwarfed in his bed, and she could see him as he had been then: standing a head taller than the rest of them. Brown-skinned with the sun and the dirt of the woods, all scabby legs and his auburn hair sticking up in tufts.

He led all the kids of the village a merry dance. He'd found the way into the Lord's private gardens and they got in without paying. Elsa could still see the flowers; the rhododendrons and snapdragons and the little bridges over the ornamental streams.

Boy Harold and some of the bigger boys had laid down in the grass, elbow deep in the cold water, trying to catch the goldfish they said Lord Rothermere had imported from abroad. The girls had stood back, laughing and keeping an eye out, gasping at the size of those bright orange fish. They were the size, Elsa thought, of my father's old boots.

'But then,' Boy Harold said. 'Remember, he threw open the gardens for free? He gave that big party on all his lawns, for all of them that were in the village. He did it for the Coronation in 1935 and we were all invited. He thought of us as his people and he invited us all. And it were music and all the food laid out on long white tables and the wine ... He'd had his cook working in the kitchen for days ...'

'Ay,' Elsa nodded. 'Except I couldn't go, could I? Cause that's when I had diptheria and me and my mother were stuck in the house.'

'That's right,' he said. 'I'd forgotten that.'

'And when I was better, after being there, stuck for months, for years, it seemed like and I could hear all you lot running wild out there in the summer, they took all of my toys and clothes and books off me and they burned them out back in the field. Remember? So the infection wouldn't spread.'

'Ay, it were cruel, really, weren't it?'

'And you laughed, you beggar! You came looking with all your gang and you were laughing at me as I watched that fire of all my things! You were dancing about and saying, Now you've got nothing, Girl Elsa. You've got no toys nor nowt, now.'

'Did I? Did I really?' He sucked in a long breath. 'Well, that's terrible. I shouldn't of.'

197

'Ay, well you did, the little beggar that you were.'

'Kids can be cruel, though, can't they?' He smiled. 'When did we learn to be different, eh? When did we learn to be better?'

'I'm sure I don't know, Boy Harold.'

'Anyway,' he said. 'I'm sorry now.'

'While I was ill and couldn't come to that big party on his lawn, Lord Rothermere sent a turkey and two big hams to my mother's house, so we wouldn't feel left out.'

'Did he? I didn't know that.'

'Two years later, in 1937, he had another party, because it was after the abdication and all the bother, and that was the one I got to go to.'

'I remember that,' he said. 'I remember you being at one of them parties.'

'Oh, and the ice cream!' she laughed. 'Remember? His cook had made it with all real strawberries, and it were out of this world, weren't it?'

'Ay.'

'And he had them ... silver salvers out on the tables, all loaded up with free cigarettes for the men. And some on them from the village, they were filling up their pockets, weren't they?'

'Ay, so was I as well,' said Boy Harold. 'I'd forgotten that.'

'You were like a grown up man to us,' Elsa said. 'King of the kids.'

Boy Harold had been the tallest and oldest in their old, tiny school. They used to catch a bus on the green and he'd lead them in messing about and fighting on the grass till the bus arrived.

'We'd have them little tatchy cases with our sandwiches in,' she said.

'I didn't,' he said. 'Girl Mum didn't make sandwiches.'

'Ay, well, we'd be so busy larking on, often we'd leave our sandwiches on the grass, because of you. We'd be rushing on the bus and then we'd be at that old school with nothing to eat.'

He laughed.

'And I remember the headmaster going to his house next door, to get his wife to make all us kids new sandwiches. That happened a few times, didn't it?'

'I can't remember. I don't remember that.'

'I do. Do you remember hiking up that hill to fetch fish and chips?'

'Girl Mum always had a craving. She loved fish and chips.'

'Biking in all weathers.'

'Did us no harm.'

'We've all lived to good ages,' she said.

'Well,' he said, 'we two have. I don't know about the rest.'

'None of them since have had to live so hard. They've not been out milking cows and what-have-you,' she said. 'I'm glad it's been easier for them since.'

'Ay,' he said. 'I reckon life's been getting easier and easier. I reckon they've all got things we'd never have dreamed of.'

'That's true.' She shook her head. 'Our Kim was laughing at me the other night, saying we were no better than savages, back then.'

'Well, she wouldn't be having her fancy life and her fancy job in that store without you. Remind her of that.'

'I think she's ashamed of me.'

'Ah, she shouldn't be like that.'

'She was saying we used to eat grass and we kept chickens in the house.'

'Well, we did!'

'I know! But at least she still came out today. She still came out to the bingo. She brung me luck. She can't be that ashamed of her poor old mum.'

'There you are, then.'

'She lives in a different world to me.'

'She's bound to, Girl Elsa.'

'I wish she was happier in it. You know when she's happiest? It's when she's on that bally computer. She's on that all night. Goodness knows what she does on it.'

'I don't understand what they do,' he said.

She could see he was worn out.

'They've had everything,' Elsa said. 'Everything what we couldn't imagine. Sometimes I think they've had it so fast and maybe so easy ... they've lived up their lives too fast and all at once ...'

'Could be,' he said.

'Well, there's something the matter with our Kim.'

He looked thoughtful. 'She probably just needs some man. She probably needs kiddies.'

Elsa raised her eyebrows. 'She won't be told that.'

'Ay. They're like that now.'

'She is. She's got her own ideas.'

'Maybe,' he said, 'she just needs a good slap.'

They laughed about this for a while.

Elsa said, 'Ay, I think it's all got faster for them. If I was young now, I wouldn't be able to keep up with all on it. I don't know how they manage to.'

'Everyone's life speeds up,' he said. 'Like what we were saying just now, about Lord Rothermere's parties, all that seems more recent and more clear than anything what's happened in the last twenty, thirty years ...'

'I reckon that's the way of it. It flies.'

'Like you wouldn't believe.'

'And you're fooled into thinking there's more time coming. You're always thinking that, because it's so fast and easy, all that time ...'

'And some on it's so boring ...'

'Ay, so you always think there's more time to come ...'

'And then suddenly it stops. Just like that.'

'Just like what?'

'Just like that,' he said.

They both laughed.

******

'Since I last came to see you, I've been thinking about all sorts of things. Really, Darren, you've got no idea what this course has been like for me. It's set my head spinning in all kinds of directions. I can't stop thinking about the things the tutors talk about in seminars. They go through my head all day long, when I'm doing ordinary things like cooking the dinner or walking the dogs. It all makes such a difference for an old woman like me.

'Oh, but I'm going on. You must have other students waiting outside to see you. You don't want to spend your whole morning listening to me rabbiting on ...'

'When I see the other students, all the younger ones, you know, I can't believe they take it all for granted. All these mind-blowing ideas. I never knew half the words they say when I was their age! Well, I still don't now! And sometimes I think I shouldn't really be here. I could be everyone's granny, but I am enjoying it, I really am.'

'Good,' he smiled.

'Even if the content is a bit shocking sometimes.'

'Ah, well ...'

'Never mind that now, I don't want to take up all of your time. There was just something I wanted to let you know about. As my advisor...'

Here it comes, he thought. 'Yes, you were saying on Saturday that...'

'I probably shouldn't have gone up to you in public like

that. On a Saturday. If all your silly students went up to you on your days off, you'd never get any peace, would you? Well, I promise I won't do it again. Was the other young man your boyfriend then?'

'No,' said Darren patiently. 'He wasn't my boyfriend.'

'I just thought I'd ask, because the two of you looked pretty thick. I hope you don't think it was impertinent of me to ask, but I know we all live in a different age now and these things are all above board and not the issue they used to be.'

'He's just a very good friend.'

'Oh, right.'

'Or used to be, anyway,' said Darren.

'Oh, there now. I've upset you. With my meddling old woman's ways. I knew I would. I do go gabbling on sometimes, like someone simple and awful. Have you fallen out, then? Is that's what's happened?'

Darren nodded dumbly and felt tears spring up in his eyes.

'Well, falling outs are just the price we pay for our good friendships, sometimes. That's how we find out what the limits are.'

'I think I've found out the limits, anyway.' His voice was thick and choked. He had to struggle to control himself.

'I'm sure it will all work out fine. Nice boy like you. Is he not of your persuasion, then?'

Darren laughed bitterly. 'Persuasion is exactly the word.'

'Oh.' She didn't understand. They looked at each other. Darren almost started to tell her more, tell her the whole story, but stopped himself firmly.

'Listen,' he said. 'We're here to talk about you. About you and your work.'

'Yes,' she said.

'You said, on Saturday, you had something to discuss with me...?'

But Elsa was elsewhere. 'You know, friendship can be a strange and mysterious thing. There's an old man I've been visiting, in the hospice. He's on his last legs. Even worse than that, probably. Well, I go and see him most every night and we talk and talk. We grew up in the same village together, all them years ago, not too far from here. So we discovered this and realised we'd known each other, back in this other life ...'

Darren nodded.

'And when I think on it, when we were daft kids and teenagers back then, I used to hate him! I thought he was too cocky by half. He made my life a blinking misery back then, saying our family was stuck up and what-have-you. I couldn't wait to be away from there and never see the likes of him and his lot ever again. And now I'm going every night and we're going through the past and ...'

'And...?'

'That's what I mean about friendship being mysterious. Where you find it, you never expected to. And besides, I think I've fallen in love with him.'

'In love?'

'Ah, now, don't look like that. Otherwise I'll think you've got a prejudice against your elders. And that you think they aren't capable of love or anything. Listen to me, saying "love" like that. I should be ashamed, shouldn't I? My daughter would be ashamed. She'd tell me I was carrying on like a silly woman, making a show of myself. Do you believe you can fall in love like that, Darren?'

'Yes,' he found himself saying. 'Yes, of course I do.'

'Good,' she said, smiling slowly.

'I'm glad for you.'

'Well, I call it love,' she said, with a sniff. 'It might just be fond. It's hard to tell when you don't see someone standing up.'

They sat for a moment in companionable silence, thinking this over.

'Is ... Is that what you came to tell me, then?' Darren asked.

'Hm?' asked Elsa happily.

'The thing that you couldn't tell your daughter about. That you wanted to tell me, as your advisor ... that you've fallen in love with this man ...?'

'Oh, goodness, no. I wouldn't bother you with that. What! Would I come to you asking after an extension on my coursework, just because I was in love with Boy Harold and I'm thinking of marrying him? Oh, no.'

'So ... what then?'

She looked almost shifty for a second. She gathered the lapels of her coat up, as if she was about to get up and go. 'No, the other thing. The other thing was ... health issues, I'm afraid. I don't want to burden you with them ...'

'No, no,' he demurred. 'You're right to tell me. We can get a note from your doctor to put in your file, just in case you're late with coursework. All the others do it. We've had the whole lot. Glandular fever, stress ...'

'I've got a lump in my breast,' said Elsa suddenly. 'I've had it for a year. I've not told Kim. I've not told anyone. I haven't been to the doctor, so I can't get a doctor's note.'

'But you must!'

'Ah, don't you get worried on my account. Sounds like you've troubles of your own. But it's kind of you to be concerned. I just wanted to tell you, because I've made an appointment with my GP this week. I've put it off and put it off. I don't know why. Silly old bird, hiding her head in the sand. That's me. But ... maybe it's because of old Boy Harold. There's nothing anyone can do to save him. He's sinking fast. Well, I'd be a fool not to see what could be done about me. So I'm going this week, to get myself sorted out. Quietly and quickly. I just wanted to let you know ...'

'Thank you ...' he said, quietly.

'So, if I was absent for a day or so, you'd know I was being seen to. Is that all right? There now, I've taken up far too much of your time. As if you want to be going on talking about some old woman's health! You should be talking to your others, all the young ones, about their essays and all that.'

Suddenly she was on her feet.

'There, then. I've told you,' she said. 'You're the first person I've told. So that's sorted out then. We're on our way.'

'Elsa,' he said, getting up. 'You don't have to rush off...'

She opened up the door and winked. Outside there was, in fact, a queue of second years, eager to talk. Elsa laughed and said, 'Just wish me luck as you wave me goodbye, Darren. Tally-ho, here I go. On my way.'

******

There was something quicker and more determined about Elsa's visit tonight. She knew that was all down to her; that she was racing Boy Harold through the pleasantries and preliminaries of their usual talk.

He lay there, all white, and she was shocked once again at the daily change in him. His breathing was much worse, having a ragged quality she didn't like at all. He was also lying flat out; she had to lean in over him so he could see her. She was gabbling away, she knew, as she told him about the day, about shopping with Kim. She hoped he wouldn't think she was racing through the visit so she could leave him again. She would hate for him to think she had better things to do.

Now she was back on going over the past and she had taken control of the narration. He watched her with milky eyes. She was talking about how she eventually came to leave the village. How it was she came to go into service, in big houses in Holt, in the old school, and then in a swanky hotel up by the coast. How her wages started at five shillings and increased only slowly, even though she was a servant to everyone.

How she slept uneasily in an attic and she was only four- teen, alone, having to learn to do everything.

He nodded at her like he knew the story already.

She described sitting in a kitchen with the maid and the cook, eating her boiled bacon and greens with them at the big, rough table. She was glad of their company.

When she thought of her working life, it seemed like, for a long time, she was alone, working alone, having to master the right way of doing things all alone. And then, gradually, she got to have company.

She'd liked polishing best of all. She liked the tang of beeswax, the clean, musky cloths, the tartness of Brasso.

'Then I went onto the land. In the war I went to Barkston, where Norfolk, Lincolnshire and Cambridgeshire all meet. I was on the farmer's land and we were beet pulling, all us girls, through the autumn and winter. We wore these big clumpy gloves. And you'd go along the rows ... I'd palled up with these girls from London. And then they billeted three airmen in the farmer's house. And that's where I met Frank, my husband.'

'Frank, was it?' asked Boy Harold.

'We used to walk into Grantham to the pictures. Other times, we'd come here on the bus. That was a long journey, though. And I loved him. I forged my birth certificate to marry him, made myself older to run off with him. It was like that. But my mother found out and there was hell to pay. But I had to get away from that village. By then, I'd seen more of the world and more people. I had Frank and I had to get away with him.'

'And leave all of us lot to ourselves in the village,' he said.

'Things were changing. That was the war.'

'People went all over the world,' he said. 'It scattered us, didn't it? Even a tiny, out of the way place like ours. It's a wonder ... any of us ever met each other again. It's a wonder we ... ever chanced on each other again ...'

This long speech left him wheezy.

'It is,' she said.

'When you think,' he mused, 'all the odds are against it.'

He had pulled the conversation back to the present moment. Their thinking-back time tonight had been quicker and shorter, too. It was exactly as if time was speeding up. Elsa's heart was flickering in her chest. As she sat quietly, biting her tongue, she felt just like a freeze frame on the telly. Still, stuck, but flickering busily.

'I want,' she said. She smiled at him again, catching his puzzled glance, so she could say it properly. 'I want us to get married, Boy Harold. Would you? I mean, does that sound silly? Like a silly old woman? But I think I do. I look at you lying in here each night and my heart goes out to you ...'

He repeated her words very carefully. 'My heart goes out to you ...' She saw he was smiling up at the Artex ceiling. 'Yes,' he said. 'I suppose my heart goes out to you, too. They must meet in the middle somewhere.'

She straightened her skirt, which was a pale, vertical-striped print. She'd had that skirt for years, she suddenly realised. She could remember handing over the money for it, in a shop that had been closed for years, back when Kim was a teenager. Really, she should have worn something new tonight, special.

'It's just sympathy though, isn't it?' he said. 'You look at me lying here. We know I'll never get out. It'll make a pretty poor marriage, won't it?'

'It will not!' she said, more hotly than she'd meant to. 'And it certainly isn't sympathy.'

He tried to sit up a little, to shuffle up on his flat pillows, so he could see her better. 'You remember me, though, don't you?' he said. 'You remember how I used to be?'

'Yes,' she smiled. 'That's what we've been talking about, all these nights.'

'So ... it's for me myself that you want me,' he said. 'Not for feeling sorry for some old man on his deathbed.'

She leaned forward and patted his cold hand.

'Aren't we ridiculous, to talk about love?' he laughed.

'Why?'

'Why ... by this stage in life we're meant to have shut up shop. Love by now is just what you feel for your family. You don't go giving it to anyone outside your family. You shouldn't be thinking about it. It's just like an ache, a pain. There shouldn't be any need for it ...'

'There is a need,' she told him.

'It'll have to be here,' he said. 'In this room. And it'll have to be quite soon, you know.'

She faked disappointment. 'Oh. And I was hoping that we'd shoot over for a weekend ... to that bally whatsitcalled ... Las Vegas.'

Clare

1

Tony had fallen into an uneasy quiet with his stepdaughter. When they talked, it was about things that had to be done now. They had a ludicrous, long conversation about ordering flowers to be sent to the crematorium on Friday. They had decided not to send something jointly and so had made two separate phone calls. Tony had managed his easily. He'd rang the local florists, up the road. Really, Clare thought, if they were that close by, he could have walked there and picked out the arrangement himself. She had listened in on him, saying the price he wanted was fifty pounds, the colours purple and white, the message simple. He had it all thought out.

He passed her the phone afterwards, as if prompting her. Well, she wasn't going to phone the same place as him. She tried a more mainstream name she recognised in the Yellow Pages. They couldn't help because she didn't have the postcode for the chapel of rest.

'Why should I have it?' she asked. 'Just look it up yourselves! I'm the customer!' But it seemed their minds were made up. She put down the phone and said, 'They were bloody useless.' Anyway, she didn't really want to order her flowers and spell out her message to her mother over the phone with Tony sitting in the same room. No, she'd find another one and do it later, closer to the time.

She still didn't know what she was going to do, to match

the fifty quid Tony was spending on flowers. She couldn't match that, but she would have to. She didn't want to have some scraggy bunch from her sat next to a sumptuous display of his.

This was how they chafed along, eating and sleeping in her mother's house. Both of them were under sufferance.

When he took the rubbish out down the alleyway, to lay in the street for the bin men, Clare had dashed out after him. She found herself asking, impulsively: 'You're not chucking out anything of Mum's, are you? I've not had a chance to look through anything yet.'

He'd looked confused. 'No. This is just trash.'

Trash? Why did he use an american word? This was just another example of him trying to appear slicker than he was.

'I want to look through her things...'

'Of course,' he said 'Whenever you feel up to it. She'd have wanted you to take something nice. Something special, to remember her by...' They were standing in the alleyway in the bright morning. He was still holding a heavy bin bag by its twisted neck. Why was she deferring to him? Letting him tell her what she could look at and take, even if it was his own house? She was her mother's next of kin. She shouldn't wait for him to tell her what she was allowed to do. She ought to take him to task. She should ask him about the will he cracked on didn't exist. She could ask him about the money.

Yet she couldn't.

These were all diversions. These were all the thoughts that came in to stop the ache in her stomach, the quick breaths and the heavy thudding of her heart as she lay awake in the back bedroom. It was like panic. Is that what grieving her mother was? Was grief just like panic and nausea? She'd never heard anyone describe it like that. With her, it was turning out to be so physical. Something, when she thought about it, she could feel all the time. Her hands were shaking. She was scared she'd make a fool of herself in front of Tony. She would look weak and make a show of herself.

It was guilt, too. They had parted on bad terms, her and Mum. There was no way to make that up now. For the past couple of years she had ignored all her mother's birthdays and Christmases. She hadn't sent so much as a card. Neither would she have sent another one until her mother came to her and said outright: You were right all along. I should never have put that bloke before you. I was wrong to.

Now Clare could never send her a card.

She'd never see her again.

Was it grief also, that made the simplest, most obvious statements like this seem so full of wisdom and real meaning? When she thought things like this, she thought she'd never heard anything so absolutely true.

She is gone forever.

The person Clare had been a week ago would have scoffed at this simple-mindedness. Now though, thoughts like this one took her ages to think and to consider.

She sat on the end of the rucked-up spare bed in the morning and thought very slowly, very clearly. Her whole life had slowed down.

2

I was a fast kid. I learned fast. I was walking and talking early. It was like I wanted to get away as soon as possible. It was always away I wanted to go.

I've got a photo, just a crumpled old snap, of Dad holding me in the garden in the first house. A washed out, late Sixties snap, him in a tank top, me in a romper suit, pebbledashing on the wall behind us. He's holding me up to the camera; it's like he's caught me in midflight. He's saying to Mum: 'Quick, Marion – take it now. While I've got her still.' Even so, I'm a bit blurred, even though Mum was quick, as prompted, with the chunky instamatic.

My hands, tiny and podgy, are clenched up, as if in frustration. I'm dying to be away again.

Don't go too fast, too far, Mum would say. She'd watch me every minute, never letting me out of her sight. Dad tried to tell her. He was sensible like that. There's no way you can, Marion. You can't keep her the whole time. You've got to let them run.

Of course, he was talking about himself there, too, though we never knew that at the time.

I never thought Mum really got over his going. That's why she got in with that slick Tony so fast. Tony was just a stand-in who ended up sticking around.

Haven't seen Dad in years. He's supposed to be in Cornwall, somewhere down there. I wonder who'll find him and tell him about Mum. Maybe he'll never know.

That thought chilled her. That there was someone so closely involved who would never know how she wound up. And he'd be free to believe she was ordinary, happy, getting on with things ... just where he'd left her.

3

They took a taxi to the chapel of rest, in a part of town neither of them knew. It was the Co-op, its windows all pebbled and opaque, the signs muted and plain. It was the kind of place they had both seen before, but had never really noticed ... eyes drawn instead to the shops either side, the newsagents and supermarkets; the kinds of places you went to every day.

And then, suddenly, came a day like this, when you had no

interest in anywhere but here and no business elsewhere. The kind of place that went on quietly at all other times, but only really existed as of today.

One of the things friends had told her about this stage in the business – this visiting of the chapel of rest – was that this made it real and brought home the truth. That's what she needed and if it hadn't been for what her friends had said (the ones who'd already lost parents and grandparents) she would never have let Tony talk her into coming here today.

At first she'd said: 'I want to remember Mum just as she was.' It was something else she'd heard someone say once. And Tony – bugger him – looked sceptical. He looked exactly as if he were thinking: You haven't seen her in years anyway. How the hell would you know what she was like?

Clare had seen the framed photos around the walls of their house. It was true, Mum had changed a little bit in the couple of years or so they'd been estranged. She had dyed her hair completely gold, instead of streaks and it was neater, somehow, more streamlined than of old. She seemed to have a few more lines, not many – but the photo she saw those in could have been deceptive. Tony and Marion had been sitting at an aluminium cafe table in the sun, somewhere abroad, last summer. It was the most recent picture Tony owned and, on it, both their faces were squinched up and more lined than they would normally be.

Inside the place was a very polite woman at a desk (what kind of woman would work full-time in a place like this? Clare wondered.) She carried on just like a doctor's receptionist, fingering the heavy-covered appointments book, checking that they could go in just yet, through the door at the side.

There was a fat, oxblood leather chesterfield, a glass-topped coffee table with pot-pourri and mints. Someone's yellow bouquet was laid out waiting on the plain pink carpet. Now Clare had started to notice details and now she was really training her attention. She was taking in everything. She felt unreal. Tony, at her side, nudging her elbow, seemed like a bogus presence. She hardly remembered who he was, standing there with sore-looking eyes, in his dark work suit.

'Do you want to go in one at a time?' he asked her. 'Or separate? You can go first, of course.'

Suddenly she didn't want to do anything of the sort.

'Together,' she told him. 'Maybe I could sit alone, afterwards.'

He nodded. The receptionist gave them a tight, bright smile. 'I'll just pop in ahead of you. I'll put the light on. Make sure she's quite ready for you.' Then the receptionist trotted off through the side door and down a quiet corridor.

'She's ready,' they were told, after a few moments.

4

Everything Clare's more experienced friends had ever told her was both true and completely untrue.

It isn't really them, they said. It's just the shell. Just the body. You can tell that the soul has already gone and this is all that's left. It doesn't even look like them.

You can feel a real presence there. You can feel them all around you. They look exactly like themselves, just peaceful. Just in a state of repose. Not a single wrinkle. All the muscles are relaxed. They look beautiful. They look very calm. They look waxy. Cold.

You can't understand why they don't react to you. Why you can't manage to make them sit up and pay attention to you, just as they always did in life. At some basic, childlike level, you really can't fathom why. They look so small, diminished, in this tiny coffin. They look huge, overbearing. This small room is filled with everything that was them.

It is like this is their ultimate face. The one they will ultimately adopt. This calm, resigned face is the one that's been waiting for them and now that wait is over.

They're peaceful.

They're angry.

They're furious.

They're pleased.

When Clare walked into that room with Tony and saw her mother, with just her face showing and all the white material pulled up around her, swaddled up like that, everything that her wise friends had ever told her came back.

And all of it was true and all of it was false. She clung to Tony.

'It's my mum,' she cried. 'It's really her. That's her.'

She grabbed handfuls of his dark work suit, and bunched them, twisted them into her fists.

'I want to kiss her. Do you think I can? Can I kiss her?'

Aisles

Rain was coming down all over Sainsbury's for Monday night shopping.

The usual thing would be for Glenda to meet Robin here at five-forty-five. She would wait where they sold videos, CDs, and magazines, at the very start of the supermarket. She would have already paid her pound's deposit for the trolley and she'd be standing with it.

He was dependable, but often late. He'd be getting the bus from campus into town. She would have brought their car. Today it was out in the far corner of the car park, glittering with rain.

Usually Glenda would have come straight from work. She'd have made the short trip from the store. And it was only now, as she watched other Monday night shoppers, fresh from work, queueing for Wednesday's lottery tickets that she realised that this was the first day of her early retirement.

*****

Glenda gave him the trolley to wheel at first. She didn't like the stiff, wonky wheels, but it turned out to be a good, well-behaved trolley. She said, 'Give it back to me. Let me push. I could do with the support.'

'Support?'

'It's the lights in here. That flickering ...'

'Fluorescent tubes.'

'They make me ... dizzy.'

'Migraine?'

'Not yet. But I could do with pushing the trolley. I could do with something to hold onto.'

'Here you go.'

He chucked a few magazines into the bottom of the trolley – computing and gardens – loving the smack of heavy, glossy paper on the wire netting.

And they went in through the automatic doors into fruit and veg. The sensors on the door were so slow they were almost clipped by them.

Soon Glenda was in the thick of picking out the usual veg. She unwound plastic bags from the cardboard tube, wetting her finger to pluck them out, finding the perforations to rip, rubbing them between her palms to make them open. Glenda never took the ready-weighed, ready-priced bags. She always picked her own. She examined each vegetable for bruising, imperfections. In the foodhall of the store where she'd worked till recently, all the fruit and veg was perfect. Robin thought it was a fascist state.

This was her first day off the job. He'd forgotten that. That was why she'd been so snappy with him. She was waiting for him to say something.

Something about freedom and had she had a nice day.

'Kim!' Glenda was saying, in a brighter, higher voice. And because Robin knew how Glenda could sound, knew all the colours of voice his wife used, he knew she wasn't pleased to see this woman. It was a frizzy-haired, bleached blonde in mumsy work clothes. She looked up from the fruit, the bright, citrus light in her face. But her eyes were tired when she turned them on Glenda.

'Kim,' Glenda said again and the two women faced each other across their trolleys.

Even Robin could see that Kim looked tired. The wonky fluorescent lights did nothing to lift her complexion. Her eyes had grey rings, like the bad bits in fish. That was her colour and pallor.

'Monday night shopping,' Kim said grimly, like it was an alibi. She was shifty, this woman, Robin was thinking. And hefty, too. An ex-workmate. He tried to recall if Glenda had ever mentioned a Kim. He was trying to snag the funny stories Glenda might have told him. Did any apply to this woman here? What did he know about her?

'I'm here with my mum,' Kim said. 'She's about somewhere.'

'Have you met Robin?'

'No.' Kim was giving him a careless look, a couldn't-care-less look. Here was a woman with concerns, Robin thought. She's hardly seeing out of those pinhole eyes of hers. She hates Monday night shopping, but there are worse things going on, that she also hates.

'Tony ... I saw Tony,' she was telling Glenda. 'I saw him last night and I met his stepdaughter ...'

'Oh, Carol ...' Glenda said.

'No, Clare,' said Kim.

'That was it.'

'She seems like a decent girl. Sensible. She's ever so upset about her mum.'

'She's bound to be,' said Glenda.

'I sat and talked with her last night,' Kim said. 'I went round to see if there was anything I could do.'

'That was nice of you.'

'I think they were pleased I had.'

Glenda nodded. 'It's all terrible. I don't know how he'll manage without Marion. He was all to pieces when I was with him.'

'He's bearing up. He'll be okay. He'll look after himself, that Tony. He's that sort. He was disappointed he hadn't seen you again ...'

'Oh?'

'Just something he said. He said you'd been a great help. You'd got him through. He couldn't have done it without you...'

'Well ...'

'But he hadn't seen you yesterday. He was at a bit of a loss. He was barely making sense...'

'That's shock.'

'Hm.'

'Shock's like that.'

'It must be.'

'At least Clare's there with him now ...'

'Hm,' said Kim. 'There's no love lost there. There'll be trouble there, I reckon.'

******

'It was my mam who used to give us peach halves straight out of the tin, and you'd have the Carnation milk with it, the tinned milk, poured over the top, sweet and yellow and creamy. You'd have it all cold, for afters. And the sweet milk would run over the peach halves into the syrup and it would separate out, like water and oil, like ... remember those lava lamps? With the moving blobs of oil all swimming about?'

'Why are you telling me this?' Glenda asked, as they pushed their way up the organic aisle.

'Everything here's all fresh,' he said.

He was such a little boy. She sighed and looked at him. 'That Kim's a bitch. She was trying to make me feel guilty for not going round to see Tony yesterday. I was round for ages on Saturday! I was with him on Friday! What right has she got to go on at me? She goes round once and thinks she's marvellous ...'

Robin gave a little shrug. 'I don't know what her problem is.'

'She's got to make other people feel crap. She's a bit sly...'

'Can we get tinned peaches, eh? I really fancy them now. And tinned condensed milk? Can we?'

She tutted at him and smiled. Glenda was used to shopping for groceries with Robin.

*****

Elsa was wandering. Kim would find her eventually in the aisles and she'd be cross with her. Kim had the list and the trolley and she would be doing her usual, orderly shopping. The only diversion from routine that Kim would permit was checking special offers. Buy three for the price of two. Otherwise, neither she nor Elsa were to be taken in by the bright, flashy produce. You could wind up spending pounds more than you'd budgeted for. It was mind-suggestion they used, as she'd had to explain, when her mother had tried to put silly unneccessaries in their trolley. It was very sophisticated and they musn't fall for it. Kim, of course, knew how retail worked.

Kim would fret that, as she was wandering abroad in the aisles, Elsa would be gathering armfuls of nonsense. Rubbishy things that had caught her eye. And Kim would just have to go round again, putting them back. Kim might even shout. She'd once hissed, louder than she'd expected: 'Do you think I'm made of money, woman?' And people had looked as she snatched some package out of her mother's hands (dips. She had for some reason wanted Mexican flavoured dips.) Kim had shoved them back on the nearest shelf and wheeled away, flushed and embarrassed. Let the stackers sort it out.

Maybe her mother was going ga-ga.

Maybe I am, Elsa thought, though she hadn't picked up any extras yet. She had barely looked at the things on the shelves. She was just wandering, getting further away from her daughter.

If Kim's not made of money, how come our phone bills are so extravagant?

Elsa hardly ever used the phone. She didn't trust it. Anyone could be listening in. But somehow Kim found time to run up these huge bills. And she paid them without any fuss or comment, so she knew they were down to her. But who was she talking to?

Elsa wondered if the phone bill could be like gas, and if that was leaking and creeping away through the underground pipes that connected your house, could that give you bigger bills? Was it like gas? Could your talk run away from you like that and seep into the ground, and escape into the air? Could you pay over the odds for talk you'd never had?

I don't really understand anything, Elsa thought. She was by the fridge freezers, she realised, and remembered she'd been sent to fetch low fat spread and skimmed milk.

Tomorrow she would use the phone. She would wait until Kim had left for work and then she would phone the surgery.

Would it turn up on the bill? Kim wouldn't let her look at the new bills they got now, but they were pages and pages long, with everything itemised. Would Kim pick it up and find her mother's single call to the surgery and quiz her about it? But bills were three monthly and there might be time. No use worrying. Kim might have to know by then that her mother had at last gone to her doctor.

She hoped the surgery receptionist wouldn't ask what she wanted to see her doctor about. Sometimes they could be nosey. They could think they were powerful. They could withold precious appointments if they thought you were a time-waster. They could refuse you there and then. I shall have to rehearse what I'm going to say, thought Elsa. And make it sound important enough, without giving too much away.

It was all very complicated. And once she made that call tomorrow morning (maybe about eleven. Not too early. They'd think she was a panicker, a hypochondriac if it was any earlier) once that was done, then there was no stopping it. All the machinery would start up. The doctor would look at her and examine her and he would tell her off. And he might even have her whisked off to hospital straight away. How would she get to tell Kim about it? Kim would think she'd ran away somewhere. Really, there was no telling what the doctor would say, when she went in tomorrow and told him.

It was like going to the police station to confess to a crime.

Low fat spread. Kim was keen on foodstuffs with things taken out. Everything on her list had some description attatched to it, telling you it had been tampered with. But tampered with for the good of your health. Kim had explained to her mother that you couldn't eat food just as it came. Not any more. They had to take impurities out. And sometimes they had to put other things in, just to keep you safe.

Complicated world.

When Kim was small she'd been a picky eater. Yet she'd grown so big. She'd been twice her mother's size since the age of ten. Elsa could remember her staring at her food at the kitchen table. Having a summer salad with the kitchen door standing open. Halfed boiled eggs, a head of lettuce, tomatoes cut into crowns. Kim had taken up the bottle of salad cream and – for badness, really - poured almost the whole lot on her sliced ham. And she'd eaten the whole lot, glaring at her mother, who said they couldn't waste good food. She'd eaten the whole mess and made herself ill. She'd been such a struggle to bring up. And Frank had indulged her. Telling her she could eat what she wanted.

It was all reversed now of course. Kim did the deciding. Elsa towed the line.

Where the milks and cheeses and margarines ended, the boxes of frozen meals-for-one began and this was where Elsa found Geoff, staring at the rows of boxes with his basket held up in front of his belly.

Ah, that's what he must eat, she thought. Those things you take out of the cardboard and prick the plastic film with a fork. The ones with sachets to pour and little compartments with a couple of potatoes, a handful of peas. How could it be enough for a big man like him? They were spinster's meals, weren't they? But, she supposed, they made shopping easier and he probably didn't have the heart to cook for himself.

He smiled at her shyly.

'Mrs Rivers, if I gave any offence the other night ... I really apologise.'

'Apologise! You silly beggar, whatever for?'

'When I was round having that takeaway the other night ... I was talking rubbish. It was that little bit of drink I'd had talking, I think. I was banging on about them burning the animals in the fields and foot and mouth, and there you were about to make yourself a nice sandwich for your supper. I'm afraid I put you right off it.'

'Oh, hush. I eat like a horse. I always have. Anyway, what you were saying was true. I do think we are heading back to the Dark Ages, the things that you hear.'

He winced and started looking at the boxes of food again. Cannelloni. Something spinach and ricotta. They seemed to organise the frozen meals by country. This was Italian food. Elsa remembered the food from her holiday with Kim.

'Is Kim still mad at me?'

'Of course not.'

'She virtually threw me out, didn't she? She kept out of my way at work today ...'

'Did she?'

'Usually ... well, quite often, we have our lunchtime sandwiches sitting together in the staffroom, you know. Well, she wasn't there today. I looked out for her. But I think she's still mad at me for my morbid talk.'

'Well,' said Elsa, inching closer to him, so that he stooped over her in turn. 'I don't know what's the matter with our Kim. She's biting everyone's head off at the moment.'

'She's not the same ...' he sighed.

'It might even be her age, you know...' Elsa said, more quietly.

'Oh, surely not.'

Elsa shrugged her small shoulders.

Geoff said, 'I wish she would talk to me about it. It must all be about Marion dying. It's got to her somehow. She must be brooding on it.'

232

'She's brooding about something,' said Elsa. 'All night long, when she sits in the spare room with that bally computer of hers. What can she be doing on that all night?'

'All night?' he asked.

'Hours and hours. I've lain awake watching the clock some nights. I've even ...' Here, Elsa looked shame-faced. 'I've even gone to the door to listen. And there's nothing! Barely a squeak out of her. Just the rattling of the keys and the occasional chuckle or mutter. They don't sound like very happy chuckles, if you see what I mean...'

Geoff was frowning heavily. It was sweet for the old woman to see. 'Do you think she could be writing a novel?' he asked. 'Maybe she's writing the story of her life...'

Elsa didn't think so. 'Not our Kim. But she is writing something, all night. Words and words and words. And she's not the type for games, either, for playing space invaders and that...'

'No, she's not.' He bit his lip. 'Is she on the Internet, do you think? I don't know much about all this, but...'

'Oh, that Web thing,' Elsa shuddered. 'I won't go on that now. I used to like it at first, when Kim showed me the patterns for knitting and crochet and all that ... they were nice things and I thought it was like magic, you know, the way you could make them print out ... but then the thing went haywire one day and I thought I'd broken it. It was flashing up all sorts of things on the screen and some of them were horrible. So I won't have anything to do with it now.'

233

Geoff took all of this in and blinked. 'I'm sure whatever Kim's doing it won't do her any harm. She's got a level head.' But he didn't look convinced at all.

'You really love her, don't you, Geoff?' Elsa asked this impulsively. Suddenly she didn't care about saying the wrong thing.

'Love?' he asked.

'You do,' she said. 'I can see it in you. When you're with her you might as well have it on your jumper, knitted in big capital letters all over your belly. I hope I haven't spoken out of turn...'

He was crimson. He was looking at the frozen meals again, as if they could cool his face down. 'I've tried to tell her. Well, I haven't. Not really. I think she'd die if I told her. Or she'd laugh in my face. And then I'd die ...'

'Tush.'

'She's much too good for me.'

'For you!'

'She's your daughter, Mrs Rivers. You know how she is. She wouldn't have the likes of me.'

He looked pathetic. He looked like he wouldn't be able to finish his shopping without bursting into tears. And I've done this to him, Elsa thought. I've reduced a grown man to this with just a few words and I never meant to. It must be so near to the surface for him. He must think about Kim all the time. I'll have to do something for him to make amends.

'You should have a better opinion of yourself, Geoff,' she said firmly. 'Kim would be lucky to get you. Yes, she's my daughter and I love the bones of her, difficult as she is sometimes. But I've told her she's a fool if she can't see what you think of her. I've told her she'd be foolish to let the likes of you walk away.'

'You did?'

'I did.'

'And what did she say?'

This was the tricky bit. He'd shrivel on the spot if Elsa told him what Kim had really said. She'd been rather unkind. But Elsa had to do something good. Life was too short not to tell white lies to good effect.

'She said...' Elsa looked into his large face and smiled. 'She said ... she knows she treats you badly. And she knows just how you feel. Believe me, she does. But she's in a bad mood just recently and she can't break out of it. She doesn't feel worthy of your love, though she pretends to be too good for it. She's waiting for you to tell it to her, straight up, and put her in that corner. I think that's what she wants you to do. Don't hedge around her. She won't respect that. Be the big man you are, Geoff and tell her right out.'

He was aghast. 'She said all of that?'

Elsa's lips went tight. What have I done now?

'More or less.'

'Do you think ... she might love me back? Deep down?'

'I've said too much.'

She patted his arm, turned and wandered away.

******

I was getting caught up in the exotic fruits.

I was thinking about what I'd said to Boy Harold the other night, about how he'd never recognise what they have on sale here. All the colours and names. How you'd never know what to do with them. Where to even start. Phyllasis. Custard apples.

I was meant to be getting the grapes and Kim was talking to that woman from her work, the husband standing by, all bored with women's talk. I was looking at the figs. Something else I'd never find a use for. I touched one and it was hard. This rind, all nubbled, and I wondered if that's what a tumour feels like.

It's in my flesh, it's not alien, my body made it, it belongs to me. It's in my breast just feeling like this and this is chilled by the cabinet. It's a dark, purplish green and that's what's in me must be like. And if they could take it out, if they could do that and slice me open at even this age I am, and carefully pull the thing out of me, it'll be just like this, like a piece of foreign fruit, all perfect and something I've grown secretly, all by myself.

******

Under the influence of one of his girlfriends - another one who hadn't worked out - John had radically altered his eating habits. When she'd been out with him in restaurants or when she'd cooked for him at home he'd laughed and said she was eating New Labour kind of food. Doing stuff for himself, he was used to having the things he'd grown up with. It was all Findus Crispy Pancakes, oven chips and Vesta chow mein with him. Now here was a world of filo parcels, oily salads, feta cheese. And this world had rubbed off on him. Mediterranean stuff, low fat, it all slipped down a treat.

Monday night and he was queueing at the deli counter and he was asking for fat purple olives and sunblush tomatoes (which looked to him like withered lips, tiny little teeth made out of seeds.) The deli counter woman was nodding at him and smiling like she was in an advert. She passed him his stacked, priced tubs. Her pork pie hat was at a jaunty angle. Perhaps she was flirting with him, but John was in no mood for it. He'd slouched out for groceries, would get a taxi back and he'd hole up at home. John didn't want to see anyone.

He'd blown everything. Cross with himself, furious with everyone else. In blowing Darren, he'd blown everything. He'd spunked the lot. Like a spending spree of friendship, he'd pissed it against the wall, all in one go. He'd spunked the fucking lot.

He still felt sexy as all hell. That's what he didn't like. He knew he looked rough, unwashed, unshaven, confused. And he resented the fact he still felt sexy and hard as hell. He'd walked away from Darren yesterday and it was like he could do anything. Everyone wanted him.

It made him feel great, made him feel like shit.

He distrusted this power Darren had managed to give him. He distrusted himself. All he could do was get away from Darren and stew over it all. Dirty little bastard, that Darren. He was behind all this. And, when he thought about it, Darren really was a dirty little bastard, actually. The kinds of things he said, they should, by rights, turn John's stomach. Just the kinds of dirty things he said in coversation, that he just came out with in everyday life any time of day. The dirty little gobshite.

But when he does say stuff like that, John thought – I just laugh. Really, I encourage him. Feta cheese, rollmop herrings. When they'd shopped together here and peered through the deli counter cabinet and when they looked together in the big store in town, Darren would say: 'Funny, isn't it – all the most expensive and flashy things to eat ... they get more expensive, the closer they come to tasting and smelling like natural bodily products and secretions. Like, the more money you have, the more right you have to taste the body itself, to actually eat it and take it in ...'

'Oh, fucking hell,' said John, repulsed.

'It's all true. I know what I'm talking about.'

'I'll tell you what puts me off about that.' John was pulling a right face. Darren had laughed at him. 'It's that tuna fish joke. You know – "If little girls are made out of sugar and spice, how come they taste like tuna fish?"'

Now it was Darren's turn to grimace.

'Well, you asked for it,' said John. 'You should count yourself lucky. Boys don't taste of anything.'

'Even dirty boys?'

'Yeah,' said John.

'How the fuck would you know?'

'Look, can we drop this? It's turning my stomach.'

'Boys can taste like anything on the deli counter,' Darren said. 'Cheese, fish, vinegar, salt. Sour tastes, sweet tastes, mostly salts. And so can girls. You've got the whole body laid out here. You can get any part of it packaged up ... All for your later delectation ...'

See? John thought. I'm best off without that kind of talk. Darren's in a world of bodily consumption and competition, in which anything can be bought and sold over the counter. He uses that phrase – disposable income – and that's what it will always be to him: just excess and what he can afford to spunk away. He'll never have a family or the need to save up for all the things that normal people need or want. He'll never have that pressure and, at this point, he's revelling in all the stupid wasteful things he can blow his money, his time and energy on. That's why he's creaming himself like a proper faggot over furniture and fittings in the Ikea catalogue, over crockery and fripperies in Habitat, over New Labour food in cafe bars and their finicky bloody menus. What he's been doing, while we've been pals, is pulling on me, drawing me into this sense of waste, of luxurious waste, for its own sake. It's a fierce, fervid pulling – a toss-off. A quick and spendthrift wank.

Like I told him, that's not my scene.

Of course, John was bound up in other bodies and a whole other sense of what they could do. The next professional qualification he was after was as a small animal surgeon. It was the minutiae of organs and stitching small, damaged hides that interested him. A different kind of sick animal altogether was what haunted his imagination. This, as he saw it, set him aside from Darren completely.

Darren had this simple, outright love for men's bodies in the abstract. They'd talked about this once. They'd decided their sexualities were the absolute opposite of each other's. When Darren considered his love of men's bodies, when he conjured in his mind his ideal erotic object, it was always male. Its features blandly perfect, depersonalised. And John said he had the same thing when it came to women. His ideal woman had a face framed with fans of dark hair. Even when he focused and really thought about it, he needn't see any specific face there. He just fancied her in the abstract and wanted her.

Fancy was a trivial word. A toss-off word. Have it once and chuck it away. Wanting was something else altogether.

He left the deli counter. He was starving now. He'd had nothing all day. The sweet–sour smells from the counter were turning him now, folding his stomach on itself with acid rumbles. He hefted his almost-full basket back down through the toiletries aisle, where he had things to pick up.

Friendship with Darren had, of course, meant that his toiletries had become poncier. Even straight gentlemen had to look after their skin. Darren had explained the requisites he needed and now he could never do without. Darren had spoiled him that way, too. John had to keep up. He'd been spoiled, over months, into competitive shopping. Into the decent, proper upkeep of a single body and self. This counted for clothes, food, furniture, magazines, CDs, trainers, digital TV channels. All of it had to be specific and right.

I'm keeping up with the fucking faggots, he thought. What a fucking freak. But I needn't. I can live it all how I want. I could have cheap clothes and fatty foods and I can sit in a house like a tip. I can revert to the contented ease of animal nature as a single, straight man. And I needn't have to try. Yeah, that'll show them. That'll show him. I'll revert, and be all the sexier for it. It's all self-indulgent crap anyway and there are more important things in life. And, what's more, one day some woman will come along and she'll decide I'll need looking after. And she'll do it all for me. That's the way it should be. Let's see what Darren thinks, when I'm no longer even trying to keep up with him.

In the meantime John had moisturisers, hair wax and assorted vitamins to buy. And it was here that he was caught by Elsa Rivers.

'Darren's friend!' she cried, in a voice that sounded brittle, like someone being cheery and false. He looked at her and groaned inwardly. They were standing by the complementary remedy jars, reading labels and the jars full of capsules and minerals sounded like maraccas in their hands. All this health, he thought, on just these shelves. It was like an arsenal of well-being in a tiny space. Jesus, he was thinking just like Darren. Thinking the same kind of analytical crap. But looking at the rows of complementary medicines gave John the same feeling as when he looked into the store rooms of animal medicines at work. All those drugs and the power they contained and could wield. They made him feel powerful. He knew how to prescribe them. That's what he knew.

'I'm seeing everyone down here this evening,' Elsa Rivers said in a syrupy voice. 'I'm bumping into everyone here. What are the chances of that, eh? All these people I know, all shopping at the same time?'

John gave her a smile and, as he did it, he knew it was sickly. He couldn't help it. She was a very insinuating old woman, he thought. The type who believed she knew everything about him at just one glance. 'It's Monday night shopping,' he said. 'It's when the shop's not too busy. It must attract a certain kind of person.'

'That's us,' she said, with a cackle. 'That must be what we are. A certain kind of person. Does that make us posh, then? Does that make us special?' She was raving. Under the fluorescent lights she looked over-excited, with two high points of red on her cheeks. He wondered if she'd been drinking. No, she was on the point of tears. Who else had she met and how had they upset her? Someone must have. He would have to be nicer to her.
'John,' he said. 'I'm John.'

'That's right,' the old woman smiled. 'Darren's friend.'

'It was outside the police station the other day, that we met. You had your dogs with you ...'

She laughed at him. 'I remember. I'm not quite senile yet.'

Now he looked at her, forcing herself to laugh and being bright like this, she reminded him of one of those old Hollywood stars in later life. Someone like Bette Davis in one of Darren's faggy films that he hoarded and watched in the early hours, making John watch as well. All that camp fucking crap. Bette Davis when she was washed up, bloated, full of drink and tar and no longer getting the plum roles, the star parts. When she was doing low budget shockers; hysterical, ridiculous, making a show of herself. That was the kind of style Elsa Rivers had settled on. No wonder Darren idolised her. Nowadays she was his favourite mature student. She was just another old hag to him.

Then John started resenting the fact that all these shite films Darren had forced him to watch had stayed such a vital part of his memory. To him his memory was a finite thing, like the hard drive on a computer. His recall for films should be taken up with the things that he really valued and the things that actually mattered in some way. He wanted to recall and replay the stuff he thought was good. Quality work like *Reservoir Dogs*, the Godfather trilogy and *The Towering Inferno*.

But when he looked in those files of his he found that Darren's stuff was there as well, all mixed up with his. The shitty low budget tat that Darren loved.

They were dead cultural artefacts from the twentieth century, still knocking about in his head. Darren loved them for their mediocrity. Their silliness. The off-kilter truths they supposedly told. But to John they had no quality, not really, these films. *The Anniversary*. *Beserk*. *Hush, Hush, Sweet Charlotte*. What a bunch of crap. Now they were filling his head, just as the music he and Darren had listened to together did. Playing itself round and round. Mondo Exotica. Batchelor Pad Royale. Bland, easy listening music. Cocktail music. Burt Bacharach and Tijuana Brass. Anything a bit kitsch. Anything without any soul. Without anything really within it. And you had to have soul, didn't you? You had to, for anything to have any worth.

That's how Darren would revere this old woman. Just another camp artefact, late twentieth century: like a cocktail bar in leatherette or a Lena Horne LP found at a car boot sale at a knock-down price. It wouldn't be for her real self at all. She was out of her time and behaving like she wasn't and Darren would love that and think it hysterical.

'Darren looks rather upset,' she said.

'You what?'

'I saw him today in his office on campus. Remember, I made an appointment to see him this morning. You were there. Well, I went to talk about a particular problem of mine ...'

'Right ...'

'And when I saw him he looked a mite upset and downhearted and he wouldn't really tell me about it. It's not my place to ask him, of course. He's the one in charge. I'm just the student. But I thought, there's a boy who needs asking. There's a boy who needs some love.'

'Oh yeah?' John could feel himself bristling.

While she rattled on, her voice all chalky and lowered right down, including him in its privacy, in imparting this confidence, he was thinking about how he could get rid of the crap Darren's friendship had filled him with. Was there some way of despatching all the rubbish you'd ever watched and talked and taken in? Could you clear space in your memory with something mechanical or medical? Could you do a make over on your memory? A *Changing Rooms* of the mind?

John just wanted to take the top-notch, quality stuff away with him, into the twenty-first century. There wasn't any time for anything else, for anything so-bad-it-was-good. That tat could fuck off. It could go to the wall.

'What, he was crying at work?'

'Not crying at work, no. He wouldn't do that. It was just the way he seemed. To me, anyway. But what do I know? I did wonder though, whether you boys had had a spat.'

'Yeah, you could say that.'

'A spat, really?'

'A bit of one, yeah.'

'Ah, that's a shame, lovey. You'll sort it out though, won't you?'

'I don't reckon we will. Not yet.'

'Ah, love.'

'It's my fault, really.'

'Is it?'

'Yeah. When I think about it. I was pretty shitty to him. Really, I didn't think I was. But I was.' Why was he saying this? What was she making him say? 'I should make it up with him.'

Jesus, those eyes of hers. All milky and blue, the red and baggy old woman's puckered skin like pleats in curtains. She was giving him all of her attention. And it was doing his fucking head in.

She was making him say things and take it all back; take all the blame. She was working some witch magic of blame on him. It was hypnotism like Alec Guinness as Obi Wan Kenobi in *Star Wars*. He was just a Storm Trooper in her hands, some dumb trooper and she could fill his mind with contrition like this.

'Poor Darren,' she said. 'You were good friends. That's not a common thing, you know. It's really not to be sniffed at.'

He couldn't tell her why. He couldn't explain what it was all about. She'd die on the spot. You couldn't explain to some old wife like this that it was all about sex. She'd never understand. She'd probably never known what that was all about. She'd have no idea at all about that.

Sunblushed tomatoes. Withered lips, dead teeth made out of dried-up seeds. And that's what he'd be having for tea tonight.

'He thinks I'm queer,' John said. 'Darren thinks I'm like him. He thinks he can be in love with me.'

Elsa Rivers nodded. 'I know. I saw that. I saw all of that.'

'And I'm not. I'm not like that. He knows it and he won't let it go.'

'He'll have to learn then, I suppose,' she said. 'It'll be hard, but I suppose he'll just have to learn.'

'Yeah,' said John.

'We can't help where we love,' Elsa said. 'And if it's like this, if it's like all this palaver ... it's not a mistake. It's an accident, but it's not a mistake.'

Who the fuck was this? The wise old woman of the western world?

'It's not something for you to fall out about,' she said. 'It's too rare for that.'

He nodded. He was offended. He was pleased.

'Love him how you can, John. Just love him how you can. Find a way, little fella.'

******

Checking out.

These are the checkouts at this time of night, without many of the checkouts busy. It's a slack night with, as Elsa Rivers suggests, only a certain kind of customer here. Those with a knack, those who know it's slack and those who want to shop in peace.

They file out gently, unloading their trolleys and baskets on the smooth rubber conveyor belts. The shop staff have been trained in expert customer service these days and every beleagured customer is greeted with 'Hello, hello and how are you?' to make them feel special. Loyalty cards are dished out for the same reason. Hey, you belong here. You're valued and recognised. And the customers are still cocooned in their privacy and sanity of their personal shopping. They are shocked into being polite.

Kim isn't, though. She knows all about customer service. John, too, is an arch consumer. He expects particular treatment. Robin, convinced of his own amateurism in his own world, expects nothing else in any other world. Glenda is past caring. She just wants the groceries unloaded, zapped by the checkout girl and loaded up again in bags and out to the car. She wants to be home. It's taken hours and hours, this. She hates Monday night shopping. She's so tired these days. Something is sapping and zapping her energy.

It's later, now. Kim has caught up with her mother at last. 'What were you doing?' Kim is perturbed that her mother hasn't been off hunting for her own kind of hopeless bargains. But she hasn't. Elsa is empty-handed. She's been wandering to no purpose. Doo-lally, after all, Kim starts to think. Maybe Mum's really flipped this time. Out wandering in the aisles. She's really gone bananas. 'Have you been talking to strangers?' Kim asks.

'I always talk to strangers,' Elsa answers. 'It's the only way you learn anything in this life.'

Kim looks at her warily. 'It's time I got you home,' she tells her.

*****

Sneaking in last of all, once almost all of the others have gone, their shopping all done and stowed away in the boots of private cars and taxis, comes Darren.

This is no surprise. Monday nights are when the boys do their grocery shopping together. This is their established routine. John came a little earlier today, though he didn't really think about the possibility of bumping awkwardly into Darren, of clashing their basket and trolley in embarrassment up one of the aisles. But that's the way John is. It isn't the kind of thing he would mull over.

Darren, however, would. So he comes later to do his shopping. He doesn't want some funny, awkward scene with John. He definitely doesn't want that.

It's still raining. It's more pissy and bleak when he turns up on foot; it's pissier and bleaker and a duller dark blue than ever and he misses doing his shopping with John.

What cheers Darren slightly is the knowledge that Monday

night is cruising night in the aisles. He knows this and John has never known it. Going later for convenience's sake might stand him in good stead tonight. He's going it alone for once. He could be a danger in the stacks; a shark coasting in the gangway.

Usually he brings John on Monday nights not only for his car, but also as a show-off gesture. He thinks – with a touch of shame now – that he was pretending to all these cruising queens in toiletries and fresh fruit that John was his fella. Hey boys, I'm taken. I'm looking round at you lot, I'm seeing what's on special offer. But I'm off the shelf. Tough luck, fellas.

Now tonight, he's thinking: back on the stacks, boy. Get yourself back on sale. He wields his trolley through the automatic doors. He winces and blinks and welcomes the many scents of the supermarket, the piped tinny muzak of oldies and standards and the flickering of wonky lights.

I'm shopping. Hey, I'm shopping alone again. And I was always good at shopping. Bargains galore.

And this is the night that Darren meets the bloke who once hunted polar bears. What are the million-to-one chances dictating that? He meets a man who camped in tents at the North Pole and guarded his home against the most savage beasts at the very top of the world.

There, the sky in spring, this time of year, is cornflower blue all day long. His stories about the arctic will thrill Darren through the night. He meets him in the booze aisle.

Darren is checking out the price of small beer. The polar

bear man (strapping, gleaming, full of himself, but in a nice way) is stocking up on spirits. That's where they get talking and making those tiny little eye contacts, the ones that add up, just as the tannoy bongs and crackles into life, alerting them that the shop's doors are closing soon.

Time to make a dash for the checkouts. Time to brave the damp, dark night.

'Come back with me and all the groceries,' Darren tells the polar bear man impulsively. It isn't the kind of thing he usually ever does at all.

Monday night shopping. You can pick up all sorts.

What a way to start the week.

******

There's just one woman left working on the tills. Everyone has to go through her. She takes her time. She's an older lady. She's one of those who've gone back into the working world and found a company willing to invest in a lifetime's experience.

She wears the proper pinny. The exact uniform. Hair's a bit messy, like she cuts it herself. Maybe she's thought of as a bit eccentric by the other girls who work here. By all the dolly birds. One thing she's not is a dolly bird.

But Iris loves working on the tills. She likes the company, likes the chat, likes all the faces she sees. She likes her fingers, nimble on the keys of her till. The great sliding of the conveyor belt.

Iris likes to know what people have in their trolleys and baskets.

You can get such a glimpse of people's lives.